Blue Midnight

Nicole Osborne

Thank you to my husband and children for always being
my biggest cheerleaders.

Chapter One

The Dream

They're after me! I can hear their heavy footsteps thundering behind me as I run, what seems like aimlessly, through the woods. The sting of branches cutting into the skin on my arms and legs as I keep running forward feel like a million needles. My lungs are on fire from the exertion and every muscle in my body is begging me to stop, but I know that I am close to safety so I can't give up. Up ahead, I can see the first rays of sunlight peeking through the canopy of trees. With the new dawn, I know my would-be attackers can't follow for much longer.

Finally, I make it into the clearing where the sunlight is breaking through the darkness and the sky is illuminated in an endless sea of pink. As I look behind me, I can see them slinking back into the safety of the cover of the trees where the sunlight hasn't yet reached. There were at least six of them and the murderous looks in their eyes promise that there is retribution yet to come.

If I could just catch my breath, I would yell out my victory, however temporary that may prove to be. Suddenly, I am overcome with a tingly sensation that races through my body leaving me feeling euphoric. I close my eyes for a moment, relishing this feeling and wondering the cause. When I finally open them, that is when I see them. Their presence brings such a sense of excitement that I feel like I haven't just been running for miles. Instead, I feel like I can hike up Mt. Rushmore in a day.

I see them both, so very different, yet the same. One has a sense of danger about him with his tousled dark hair, very built physique, and piercing blue eyes. His sexy grin just makes me want to run into his arms and never let go. Just looking at him has my body feeling like it has been hit with lightning. But then, there is the other one.

His gentle smile and quiet beckoning makes me feel like I am finally home. He looks at me with such hope in his chocolate brown eyes that I feel torn inside for yearning for the other. He stands a little taller than the other one and is just as fit. I can't make up my mind what to do when I hear the piercing sound. It is all around me like it is a part of me, yet I can't figure out what it is or where it is coming from.

I abruptly woke up, covered in sweat from my dream, only to realize I was going to be late for work again if I didn't shut the alarm off and get up. The dream is always the same. I consistently seem to wake up just before I get to the good part. Just once, it would be nice to make it to the juicy part and feel that all this angst is worth it. I have had the dream since I was about sixteen but ever since I graduated from college a few months ago and turned twenty-one, the dream has haunted me almost every time I close my eyes. I feel like it has to mean something but what?

I slowly drug myself out of bed to shower and get ready for yet another day at work. I earned a degree in journalism with a minor in English so I could write my own books, not edit other people's work, but I guess I have to start somewhere. After I was nearly ready to leave, I looked one last time to assess myself in the mirror. My blonde hair was in its signature work updo. My heavy lashes framed my bright green eyes and looked startling against my pale smooth skin. I could probably use a little sun. I still work out all the time so even though I am petite, I am fit. Mom got me into working out long before she passed away. I think I keep up with it just to feel closer to her, plus I really enjoy chocolate so this way my addiction doesn't mess up my figure.

My life has never been simple. My mother passed away due to cancer soon before my eighteenth birthday. It still hurts everyday and although I have moved on, I will never forget her or stop missing her. It is like a piece of my heart is missing that can never be replaced.

I moved out on my own as soon as I could. Once we lost my mom, my dad became an insufferable, miserable old man. He didn't want to be around me and he wouldn't allow me to help him out. He always gave me the impression that he detested me and that became greater once mom had passed away. He took great pleasure in shutting me out of his life. He never appreciated how close my mom and I were and I always thought that he felt like I took her time away from him. We always tried to include him, but he never wanted to be included. I never saw much affection between the two of them. Most of the time, I marveled at why my mom ever married him to begin with, but whatever.

The entire situation with my dad has made me very picky when it comes to men. I don't care to date anyone if I feel I am wasting my time. I definitely do not want to end up with someone who resents his own child or doesn't make time for me or our children.

I worked as a waitress throughout college so I could tuck as much money away as possible and have a place to live once college was over. It wasn't the world's greatest job but it helped me save just enough to rent a cute little one bedroom cottage. The place literally looks like something out of a fairy tale with a porch that wraps around the entire home, cute little picture windows in the front, and a cozy interior with a fireplace that keeps me warm in the winter. The only hitch was that it is so far away from everything, it takes forever to get to work or to go anywhere.

I still own my old Toyota SUV from when I was in high school. It was the one gift dad begrudgingly gave me and it has lasted me a long while, even if it does look like a soccer mom vehicle.

Working all the time doesn't give me much time for a social life, which quite honestly, is just fine with me. I enjoy my quiet time and have never been much of a people person; I never quite fit in anywhere.   My life consists of either writing or working. The only time I get out is when my friend Lindsey drags me out somewhere.

She has been my friend since I was fifteen and moved to dreary Ohio. No offense to those who love Ohio, but after living in California most of my life, Ohio is kind of a drag. We moved to an area where there just isn't much going on, ever. The biggest excitement around here is wondering who you might see at the mall on the weekend.

When I graduated from college, I had big dreams of writing my own book but the only job I could find was as a book editor. It gives me an advantage while I am writing my own books since I know what sells and how to edit. It will eliminate a lot of costs when my book is ready to be published. It is not that I mind my job, it's not a difficult job and I get nine to five hours and weekends off, which is a first for me. It just wasn't what I thought I would have at this point, but I am slowly working on my own book in my free time. Hopefully, when I am finished, I can get published and someone else will be editing my books for a change.

I moved through my work day as I always did, getting caught up in editing books and avoiding certain male co-workers who can't seem to get the hint that I don't want to go out. There is a tiny little cubicle that I call my home away from home. It has white partition walls, a desk, my laptop, a very comfortable soft leather chair, and little else. A picture of my mother sits on my desk, which is the only thing that I have done to make the cubicle my own. I don't really see the point in making this space homey. That is what my actual home is for.

Everyone else has their cubicles decorated and containing pictures of significant others or children. Since I don't have either, the choice not to decorate seemed a simple one for me.

When I am editing, it feels like the entire world drops away and it is easy for me to ignore the buzz going on around me. I am kind of a loner so tuning out the world is fairly easy for me.

At the end of my uneventful shift, I was a bit tired. It is funny how reading and editing all day can actually make someone tired. It is not a physically demanding job, but mentally I feel like I need some time to unwind by the end of the day.

I decided to order a salad and head home. I rarely bother with grocery shopping so it is easier for me to just grab something on the fly. When I was at the restaurant waiting for my salad, I started to feel that familiar tingling I feel as I do in the dreams I have. It made absolutely no sense at all. One minute I was tired and tense thinking about all the things I needed to do when I got home, and the next I felt this wave of overwhelming excitement. Out of the corner of my eye, I would have sworn I saw one of my dream guys. Not the sexy one with penetrating eyes, but my other guy whose mere look in his eyes welcomes me home. I turned my head so fast to look I nearly knocked the table on its side. As fast as I thought I saw him, he was gone. My cheeks were burning with embarrassment, no less than ten people saw me almost upend the table. I smiled sheepishly and said, "Bad day." Everyone just either shrugged or stopped looking.

I was silently chastising myself for my foolishness when my name was called because my food was ready. As I walked slowly toward the pickup shelf, I kept glancing at those around me, looking for the man I thought I saw. I watched two children running through the throng of people waiting patiently for their food by the stand. There were a lot of people in deep conversation and one person at the counter who was apparently not happy with the prices and was making sure the cashier knew how she felt. The one person I was looking for was nowhere to be found. I probably imagined him; editing fiction all day had fried my otherwise logical brain.

I made it to the counter and thanked the kid who made my food and was just making my way back to my car as my phone vibrated. My friend Lindsey, who is as wild as a summer storm, wanted to go dancing and wouldn't take no for an answer. All I wanted to do was go home and relax, but she was hard to say no to. She was giving me a whole thirty minutes to get ready once I reached my home, which was not nearly enough time. I just managed to get home and shower, put my wet hair in a towel and put on my black skirt and super cute shirt when she rang the doorbell.

As soon as I opened the door she took one look at me and breezed past. "Are you seriously not ready to go yet? That's it. I am doing your hair and makeup so we can get out of here and go dancing." That, of course, was said and she began dancing around my house and gathering everything she would need to make me what she called *beautiful and ready to find Mr. Right or at least Mr. Right now.* Lindsey was very tall but very pretty with high cheekbones, long brown hair, a slender body, and a personality that had men draping themselves all over her. I was definitely more low- key. After twenty minutes, she declared me ready to rock so we were out the door.

"I need this night so badly. My whole week has been shit. My boss is on vacation and the jerk that he left in charge is on a major power trip. So, how is the book editing going?"

"Same old, same old really. I like the job and it pays the bills but all I want to do is write my own books, but I spend so much editing other people's books it doesn't leave a lot of time. So, what happened to Robby?"

"Robby was last week. I am so over him. I could not stand to watch him eat. It was like watching someone take a shovel and inhale all of their food. He had to go."

All I could do was laugh. She never kept a boyfriend for very long. The longest she ever seemed to be able to stand a man was an entire month and that was over because he wanted to watch an action movie. She always found the most trivial reasons for getting rid of her men but that was just her, and to know her was to love her.

Chapter Two

The Night Out

When we finally made it to the bar, the line to get in was wrapped halfway around the brightly lit building. Everyone in line was either chattering about how greta the bar is or taking selfies or sending snapchats. I inwardly groaned. Why did I agree to this? I could be relaxing at home and working on my book instead of standing in line with a bunch of already drunk and obnoxious people. When I started walking toward the back of the line, Lindsey gave me a wink, grabbed my arm and started pulling me to the front. We walked past a lot of people who were yelling out to us to stop and others who were complaining about us trying to skip to the head of the line. Lindsey seductively sidled up to the door guy and flashed her brightest smile so we didn't have to wait in the long queque. I am pretty sure she gave him her number too. I shouldn't be surprised, that was classic Lindsey.

The bar was immense with a dance floor that seemed endless. The energy from the band that was playing had the entire bar enthralled and pulsating to the music. It was the only bar in town that wasn't considered a dive bar. It was also the only one with a dance floor that had an upper and lower level large enough to accommodate over a hundred party goers without anyone bumping into each other. The lights were low, with the exception of the light show that showered over the dancers.   The colorful lights blinked in and out to the beat of the music. Everyone was already crowded onto the floor moving rhythmically to the beat. The one thing I love to do besides writing is dancing. It takes my mind off of everything to just give myself over to the music.

We made our way through the throng of revelers to the middle of the dance floor and allowed the music to flow through us and take over. The song was very upbeat and we were having a great time already. The lights were flashing in and out of existence in their intense colors, adding to the festive mood.

I was startled by an eerie feeling that I was being watched and glimpsed around. My eyes landed on the most beautiful man I had ever seen. He looked like a Greek God that had been sculpted by the heavens. At first, he reminded me of a young Tom Ellis, the mouthwatering man who plays Lucifer on t.v. You could see his muscles pressing against his shirt and his eyes were so penetrating that I felt mesmerized. He seemed very familiar and it finally hit me that he looked exactly like the man from my dreams, but I knew that wasn't possible. *Was it?* Sexy blue -eyed guy was walking toward me, like right out of my fantasies. I shook my head to clear it and looked again and he was within inches of me. He boldly grasped my hand and kissed the back of it as Lindsey and I stood there with our mouths gaping. I am sure it was not my best look. Lindsey was the first to snap out of it and asked me to introduce her to my friend. I grasped for words but nothing would come out. I probably looked like a fish that had just been caught on a fisher's line, gasping for air. Blue eyes, still holding my hand, turned his attention to Lindsey.

"I'm Alaric. Pleased to meet you....???"

"Lindsey."

"Of course, Lindsey. Well, Lindsey, if you don't mind I am going to steal your friend here for a moment."

Just the timber of his deep voice had me salivating. Lindsey gave me a look that was difficult to decipher. For just a moment, she looked like she was a kettle that got too hot and began to boil over. The look was so fleeting that I almost wondered if I imagined it. In the next instant, she gave me a sly grin and waved us off to have fun. I watched her walk stiffly off the dance floor and over to the bar for a drink. I would have to ask her about the strange attitude later. Right now, I had a sexy guy to dance with.

A slow dance began pouring from the speakers. He pulled me into his arms near the edge of the dance floor and began slowly moving to the music. He had an air of confidence about him, but why wouldn't he? I am sure no one had ever turned down a dance with him or anything with him for that matter. I stared up at him as the warmth of his hand seemed to burn a hole through the back of my shirt. He gazed back at me, so self -assured and alluring.

"So, you look like you've seen a ghost."

Finally finding my manners and my mind I said, "I am so sorry. You just remind me of someone. My name is Phoebe."

"Well, I hope it is a good someone," he said in his sexy deep voice that could melt butter.

He was silent after that but kept gazing into my eyes as we danced. I could not seem to look away. So, I was in Alaric's arms swaying to a song I can't really hear because my mind is cluttered with the reality that I must be having some kind of psychotic break. A man that I have been dreaming about for as long as I can remember doesn't just walk out of a dream and into my arms on the dance floor. I reluctantly stopped looking at him and looked around at all the other couples. Everyone seemed absorbed by the music, except one couple who seemed to be arguing. I could see Lindsey sitting by the bar with a drink in her hand and a scowl on her face. I must be dreaming this whole thing. So, I decided to just go with it. If I was losing my mind, I may as well enjoy it.

I laid my head against his shoulder as I felt his powerful arms encircling me. He was taller than me by at least a foot. He had dark hair that hit the bottom of his neck and was so silky I wanted to run my fingers through it. He had an amazing smile and deep blue eyes that reminded me of the ocean on a beautiful sunny day. He had a manly scent of sandalwood and sunshine and I just wanted to spend the rest of my life here breathing in his exotic scent. He was wearing dark pants and a white button up shirt that hung open at the throat, and what a sexy throat that was.

I looked up at him and wondered how this could be happening to me. He just gave me a sexy grin and stared into my eyes. I don't know what made me do it but I asked why he decided to finally come and meet me. What had he been waiting for? When he didn't seem too shocked by my question, I knew I was inside some alternate reality. That new guy at the restaurant definitely put something in my food and I was probably passed out on the floor of my house in a puddle of my own drool. He quirked his eyebrow as he presumably contemplated how to answer me.

Alaric said, "It wasn't safe until now. I had to make sure you were going to be ok. I had to finally be in your life, no more sitting on the sidelines and watching. Since you know who I am, I assume that Xander already got to you first and explained the kind of danger you are in. He told me he was going to wait and just watch to make sure you were safe but I guess he lied to me."

I didn't have any time to fully absorb what he was saying. The moment I looked into his eyes, everything he had just declared became like white noise in the background and the meaning of it all floated away into nothing. He must have sensed that I was not capable of listening and gave me the most lustful look I have ever seen on a man's face. Before I had time to react, he brought his hand down to caress my cheek and as we swayed to the music. He bridged the distance between us until I could feel his breath mingling with mine. His lips were mere centimeters away from mine and I closed my eyes and waited for his kiss. I didn't expect to feel the onslaught of emotion that unleashed. I felt like I needed to be as close to him as I could. The whole dance floor melted away and it was just him and I clinging to each other like our lives depended on it. He was the life preserver and if I didn't hold on tightly enough, I may drown.

As we kissed, I began to see flashes in my mind that didn't make any sense. I could see myself standing outside my high school getting into my car. Flashes of me walking onto campus where I took my classes and flashes of my life for the last five years. Why was I having these flashbacks as I was kissing the most gorgeous man I had ever met? The bursts of the past looked like photographs taken from afar, not memories of my own. This is not what I expected when we started kissing. What did this all mean?

The flashes stopped in an instant and I just kept kissing him, sure that I was going to go up in flames from the passion, until I heard someone clear their throat behind me. I broke away and looked to see his eyes glazed over from our make out session and Lindsey standing behind him looking a little pissed off. The slow song had apparently ended half of a song ago because it was halfway through a different and not at all slow song. She said excuse me to Alaric and not too elegantly pulled me away to a table just off the dance floor. I was too stunned to protest. He stood across the room just waiting for me. She started grilling me about him.

"Who was that?"

"That is Alaric." I said as if that explained everything.

"How long have you known him?"

When I failed to answer her, she continued her interrogation. "Exactly who is *Alaric?*" She spoke his name as if just saying it left a bad taste in her mouth.

That is when reality really kicked in and I realized that I was not dreaming. He was there...really there. I had just kissed a total stranger that I had been dreaming about for years. This was insane! I had to get out of there. None of this made any sense.

Lindsey grabbed my arm and gave me a little shake like she was trying to shake some sense into me. I just could not deal with any of this right now. I pulled my arm away and without another word, I bolted for the door. I knew it wasn't logical but I felt that I was suffocating and I needed to get home, drink a glass of wine, and put this whole thing behind me because clearly, I was crazy. I was mildly surprised when neither Lindsey or Alaric tried to follow me and stop my dramatic escape.

Lucky for me, there were always taxis outside the bar ready to take home the people who were too drunk to navigate their own way there. I got into one and I was driven home. The taxi smelled like cigarette smoke and weeks old gym socks but it was better than the alternative of being at that bar and thinking I was losing my marbles. I had so many things on my mind that I don't even remember the drive home. I kept alternating between differentiating scenarios. One scenario was that I just thought the guy looked like my dream guy and I had made a total fool of myself by kissing a complete stranger. Another idea I had was that I had met him before or had seen him before and that was why I had dreamed about him. The last scenario was that I was on the brink of insanity.

When I got home, I paced and drank and paced some more. Lindsey tried to call me several times but I let it go to voicemail. I just couldn't face whatever it was that was happening. She had such judgment in her gaze when she was asking me about him. Dealing with her was the last thing on my agenda at the moment. Since I had no way to make sense of this entire evening myself, I could not even begin to try to explain what I was feeling to my friend.

By the time I got to bed, I had rationalized that this guy I kissed and danced with was just some random man I met and didn't at all resemble the dream guy. The lights in the bar were low and he just had some kind of resemblance to him and because of that I threw myself at him. It still didn't explain why I saw flashes of myself at various stages of my life while I was kissing him so I tried to not think about that part of the evening.

I was mortified and would eventually have to explain this to Lindsey. I felt terrible for just taking off like that. It wasn't like me at all, but I just felt so overwhelmed, I had to leave. I just hoped I would not run into this guy again, but it did make for a nice memory. The man could definitely kiss! I also hoped with everything in me that I would run into him. I just needed to stop thinking about the entire night, go to bed, and forget it ever happened.

Chapter Three

Normal?

Life went on as normal for the next few weeks. I still had the dreams and I had to explain to Lindsey about the guy from the bar. She basically said I should have just gone for it and she shouldn't have freaked out so much. She was just worried that night because it was so out-of-character for me to make out with a complete stranger. For several weeks, I didn't see Blue Eyes after that night, except in my dreams. I had finally reached the point where I was sure I had dreamed the entire thing when Alaric walked into my workplace in the middle of the day.

I was walking back to my office from lunch when I got that familiar tingling going up my spine. I turned around and there he was, asking the receptionist if he could see me. He hadn't yet spotted me and I considered making a run for it, but decided that I needed to face this, and besides, he was very attractive. I stopped and took a deep breath, turned toward the reception desk and let Lola off the hook. Actually, after looking at her I am not sure if letting her off the hook would be the right phrase. She looked like I had just run over her dog when I began escorting him to my office. Her eyes trailed after him and the look on her face showed she was debating on running after him. I could understand the attraction. He was definitely swoon worthy. He looked even better in the light of day. His hair was definately silky and I had to stop myself from reaching out to touch it. His skin was flawless and he had a little bit of stubble making him look rugged and dangerous.

"How can I help you?" I asked him wondering in the back of my mind if I was having another psychological break. In the light of day there was no mistaking it, he looked exactly like my dream guy. Trying to be logical about this, I thought that maybe I had seen him when I was younger and that my subconscious injected him into my dream.

"We have an appointment in about five minutes," he replied, looking at me expectantly. It took me a moment to shake away the cobwebs that were clearly filling my mind, and I inclined my head for him to follow me.

The entire way to my office, I was trying to stave off a panic attack. *How does he know where I work? What does he want?* It cannot possibly be to discuss what happened weeks ago at the bar. We walked into my office or what is more like my cubicle. We walked past plenty of admiring females along the way and many more men who were scowling at him. Aside from my high heels clicking on the tiles as we walked, it seemed there was a hush in the building and all eyes were on us.

When we reached my cubicle, I indicated a chair for him to sit in and I sat across from him. "What can I do for you?"

"Well, I had no idea that you were the one that I had met a few weeks ago until I walked in here today. What a wonderful surprise. I am actually here because you are editing my book, I believe, and your boss wanted you to meet with me to give me some feedback." He looked at me expectantly.

That is when I put the pieces together, he was Alaric Richmond. I was editing his book. Actually, it was difficult for me to put it down just to leave for lunch and home the past couple of days. It was captivating. It was a paranormal novel about vampires and a woman, who had no idea she was even a vampire. It sounds a little crazy and it is not the usual book I get excited about, but this one had so many twists and turns, that I found myself thinking about it even when I was away from work.

So, Alaric was not only gorgeous and a great kisser, he was also a talented author. He sounded almost too good to be true. I began to recall the events from a few weeks ago and I was sure my face was going up in flames. I tried to regain my composure. This was *"work Phoebe"*, not *"going out and kissing strangers at bars Phoebe."* I sat a little straighter in my chair and crossed my legs. He noticed the movement and gave my legs more than a passing glance which only made me want to blush again. I picked up the copy of his manuscript and held it in my lap.

"Well Alaric, I have been editing your book. I have to say that you are quite talented. This is not the genre that I usually edit, but I was pleasantly surprised by your novel. It has me intrigued and it takes a lot to do that after editing thousands of books. I have to wonder what your readers will think of a woman who has no idea what or who she is. I believe that we have a growing market for this and that it will be successful. I am still not through with the process but will be soon. I really don't have too much feedback for you. Usually, I would have a lot to suggest but this is really good so far. I am not sure why my boss called the meeting." I felt a little perplexed. I usually didn't meet with the authors directly. It was highly unusual to have a meeting in person for feedback. I usually never talked this much or this fast in my life, but he made me very nervous. I sat back, took a deep calming breath and decided to let him take the lead on this.

"I'm glad to hear it. This is my first novel and I was very nervous about meeting with the editor. I was afraid you were going to tell me there was no chance that my book would be worth your time." The way that he looked at me had me fidgeting in my seat. He looked like he was undressing me with his eyes, even though his words were all about business.

"Quite the opposite. I look forward to finishing up this process for you so the book can get out there. I am sure you will have a huge fan base in no time." I could imagine all of hiws book signings and all the fans draping themselves over his deliciousness. I felt a pang of jealousy over the uninvited imagery. I had no claim over him but I wanted to. It wasn't just his beautiful visage, or even the way he had kissed me senseless. I could eventually forget about those things, maybe. There was something about him that drew me in like an invisible cord. I wanted to know more about him. I wanted him to be mine.

"In that case, can I invite you to dinner to help me celebrate my upcoming success?"

I wanted to say no. I wanted to scream yes. My mind was doing somersaults and I wasn't sure if I was going to give him an answer or faint at his feet. I tried not to think about the fact that I had made out with him at a bar a few weeks ago, or that I had been dreaming about him nightly, or even the fact that this gorgeous man wanted to take me to dinner. I was afraid that I would do or say something that would make him want to turn around and run. I wasn't the dating type. I was the stay- at -home with a good book type, but of course he didn't know that because I was throwing myself at him weeks ago. Was it even a good idea to mix business with pleasure?

I looked up into his alluring eyes and it looked like my answer was very important to him. I decided that anything good was going to be a bit complicated but completely worth it. "That would be great. Where can I meet you? I am off work at five."

We both stood up and suddenly the cubicle was way too small for both of us. We were standing so close that I could feel his body heat like a warm blanket on my cold skin. He picked up my hand and kissed the back of it. "I will pick you up here at five. Until then..." With that, he turned around and began walking away. He even looked good from that angle. All kinds of lascivious thoughts were going through my mind and I was sure I was staring at his backside when he turned around and gave me the sexy sideways grin. At any moment, my entire body was going to become engulfed in flames. How can he do that with just one little look?

As soon as he left, three female co-workers cornered me.

"Who was that?" Jasmine asked while fanning herself. They all looked at me expectantly. Jasmine was a young and curvaceous blonde who worked in my department. She looked like the type of woman that Alaric would take out on a date, not me.

"That was a client. I am in the process of editing his novel and he came here to ask for some feedback."

feedback anytime." Charlotte said. She was very short and with thin brown hair and I was pretty sure very married as well. All three of them giggled like school girls and walked back to their own little cubicles. I really couldn't blame them. I felt like a school girl with her first crush waiting for the boy of my dreams to take me out on a first date.

I sat down and began to ponder just what I had gotten myself into. Yes, he was beautiful with those high cheekbones, tight muscles, and striking blue eyes but why did he seem interested in me? I considered myself decent looking and I stayed in shape but I was not a man magnet by any means. I felt very ordinary next to him. He looked like he belonged on the cover of a magazine.

The attraction was there, it seemed on both sides. I was still a little embarrassed at how I practically threw myself at him that night and then panicked and fled. I wondered what he must be thinking about me right now. *Was the evening an official date or did he just want to pick my brain about his book?* I guess time would tell . I also had more than a few burning questions about our short conversation that we had that night. *Who was Xander and what kind of danger was I in? Why did I see flashes of myself when I kissed him?* None of that had ever made any sense to me and as time went on, I had begun to feel that the whole thing had been a hallucination but yet here he had been, in my office, and he would be back at the end of the day to take me out. I needed a diversion before my brain melted from overthinking it all.

I busied myself by reading his book to take my mind of the evening. I tuned the rest of the world out, as always, and concentrated on my work. There were a few errors here and there that I had to work on, but the book was phenominal. I couldn't even describe it, but it was one of those books that actually made me feel like I was there and could feel what the characters were feeling. It took me into an alternate reality where vampires were real and even made them seem just like any ordinary person with some extraordinary powers. I felt a kinship with main character, she had lost her mother as well and felt a little lost.

Before I knew it, the time was a quarter to five and I needed a few minutes to freshen up before I would be ready to meet Alaric. Even his name sounded exotic. I definitely had never met anyone else with that name. I walked to the restroom with my purse and dug out some lipstick and some powder. I decided to take my hair out of the updo and let it flow down my back. I added some lipstick and powder and after one more look in the mirror declared myself ready to take on Alaric.

There was a nervous energy thrumming through me on my walk outside the building. I was equally excited to see him again and just as nervous that I would say or do the wrong thing. I walked to the parking lot and he was sitting out front in a Mustang, of all things. It was my favorite color blue, like a Caribbean blue. One more point in Alaric's favor. I took a deep breath and mentally prepared myself for the evening ahead.

As I approached the passenger side of the car, he got out and opened the door for me. That was such an old fashioned but chivalrous gesture that I felt like a queen. "I am glad you decided to go to dinner with me. You look lovely."

"Thank you." I said as I blushed profusely.

"So, are you in the mood for Chinese food, Italian, or Mexican?" He said as he quirked his brow at me. I told him Chinese food is always my go-to and he hesitantly closed my door, got into the driver's seat and we headed away. He looked like he was made for that car. He was equal parts dangerous and powerful.

"I am almost finished with your book. I haven't had to make too many changes. Of course, I am just the developmental editor so it still has to go through the copy editor and proofreader. I did a little of what the copy editor does and fixed a few grammatical errors though. I haven't seen any plot holes or anything that needs to be changed to make it marketable. It really is fascinating and I can't wait to find out how it ends. What gave you the idea to write this?"He smiled in a way that was mysterious and made me want to figure out his secrets. "Thank you for editing it for me. I am really grateful and looking forward to having it out there. I am really glad you are enjoying the story."

He never really answered my question about how he came up with the idea when we pulled into the parking lot of a posh Chinese Restaurant. He parked and cut the engine and was around to open my door before I had a chance to even gather my purse. He gallantly offered me his hand. I swear every time he touched me that a jolt of electricity and awareness would thrum through my body. I wondered if he could feel it too.

I had never been to this restaurant before because of the price. It was candle lit on the inside and the tables were set up in a way that made each seem like their own little private island. There were linen table covers and a rose on each table in cute little crystal vases. Alaric slipped the hostess some cash and got us a table way in the back that appeared like it was reserved for special guests. It was so far out of the way it seemed like it had a zip code all its own. We would not be disturbed and that both gave me a shiver of anticipation and made me a little nervous at the same time. The hostess didn't seem like she wanted to leave. She asked Alaric twice if there was anything else she could get for us, but she really meant him. I was surprised she wasn't giving him her number, but the night wasn't over yet.

He didn't seem to notice the hostess much which really surprised me. Most men would be soaking up that kind of attention like a sponge in the ocean. He just thanked her and she walked away looking like a pouting five year old. Thankfully, our waiter was a man so I didn't have to deal with another woman throwing herself at him. Not that he was mine, I had no claim, but it was a little annoying nonetheless. The waiter took our drink orders and disappeared. Alaric moved closer and leaned in before asking me how my day was at work. It was impossible to think with him in this close proximity. I could feel his warm breath fan against my cheek. I had never really had anyone who asked me how my day was, not even my friend Lindsey so the question took me a moment to answer.

"Everyday is the same really. I read other people's books and look for plot holes or poor character choices and try to correct them. Your book is the first that really has me looking forward to going back to work tomorrow. I enjoy my work, please don't misunderstand." I kind of put my foot right in my mouth. He made me forget that he is a client. He probably wanted to hear that my job was fascinating and I loved every moment.

"So, what do you enjoy, outside of work, that is?"

"I am writing my own book that I have been working on since I graduated from college. I just never seem to have enough time to really focus on where my story is taking me. Then, there is Lindsey always trying to get me to go out. She is a whirlwind. Every time I am out with her I have a great time but I also have the feeling I am inside a tornado about to get swept away if I am not careful. She just has this energy about her and usually the guys are draping themselves all over her while I enjoy dancing. Even when we go out shopping, it seems that she can't help but attract all sorts of attention. There is never a dull moment. How about you?""Oh, my life is pretty boring really. I spend a lot of time with my family when I am not working on my book. I used to work as a high school teacher but I realized after a few years that it wasn't where I really wanted to be."

First of all, I could not imagine that his life was in any way uneventful. I don't know why but I felt a warmth at the idea that he is a family man.   I briefly wondered if maybe he was married. He was interesting, unbelievably gorgeous, and talented as an author. I couldn't imagine someone not snatching him up right away. My thoughts were trailing away and I didn't even realize the waiter was ready for our orders.

We ended up having an amazing dinner and the company was even better than the food. I wanted to ask him more about the first night that we met, but something had me keeping those questions to myself. Maybe I didn't want to ruin the evening, maybe I was afraid of losing a client, but mostly I was sure that the magic of it all would disappear the moment that I found out the truth.

When the evening was over, he drove me back to my car and opened the door for me. He hesitated like he wasn't sure what his next move should be. *Had this just been a business dinner or had it been a date? Would he kiss me or should I shake his hand and wish him success with his book?*

"Well, I am sure you wondered if I asked you to accompany me to dinner because you are my editor. The truth is, I have not been able to stop thinking about you since we met that night. I wondered where you went and I never got your number or had a chance to meet with you again. I believe it is fate that brought me here today and found that you are the one editing my book. I would very much like to see you again."

His declaration took my breath away and I was at a loss for words for a moment. I believe he took that as a rejection when he began to step away.

"I am sorry. I obviously overstepped."

"No, not at all. I guess I just wasn't prepared to hear that. I would very much like to see you again."

With that, he stepped forward so fast I didn't even see him make a move. I was in his arms. He leaned forward and our lips brushed, and I was certain the friction caused a spark. We both looked at each other and he deepened the kiss. I was swept away in a sea of emotion. While the first kiss caused a spark, I was sure this one was going to cause an explosion. I didn't think, I could only just feel. Too soon, he ended our kiss and I realized I was still clinging tightly to him. We were both a little breathless and I really didn't want this evening to end but I didn't know him enough to invite him to my home. The temptation was still there but his next words took the choice out of my hands.

"I should be getting home. I had an amazing evening. I will call you here tomorrow and we can make plans." Too soon he was in his car, and roaring out of the parking lot. I hadn't even had a chance to respond back to him. It was like he couldn't get out of there fast enough. Was the kiss not as powerful for him? Ugh! I just needed to go home, take a cold shower, and curl up with a good book.

All the way home, I was trying to think about the date with Alaric but I kept having this nagging feeling that I was being followed. It was so strange because not many cars were on the roads out where I lived. This silver Volvo was behind me, but it kept its distance. I began to wonder if maybe I shouldn't go home but take a detour just to make sure I was not being followed. Once that thought entered my head, the car passed me. I shook my head. I really was beginning to get paranoid.

Chapter Four

Is This Reality?

That night, I dreamed the same old dream, only this time it ended differently. Once I was out of the forest and entered the clearing, both men were still there and I felt the same fluttering, tingling feeling but this time I knew my destination. I walked right up to Alaric confidently and he hugged me tightly and began kissing me as the rest of the world fell away.

I woke up with thoughts of Alaric dancing in my brain, and I couldn't help but smile. I couldn't wait to get to work so I could read his book and anxiously wait for his call. I felt like a school girl waiting on a boy that I had a crush on to call me. The butterflies in my stomach felt like they were building a permanent home.

All morning, I had that nervous energy. It made me feel restless and my limbs felt as thought they were buzzing with electricity. The call finally came at lunchtime. The moment I heard his sexy voice on the other end of the line, I couldn't help closing my eyes and picturing him there with me. All the anxiety flowed out of me and I was left with a feeling of elation. I was floating on a cloud.

" I would really like to meet you for coffee tomorrow. *Just Java* is a great place. What do you think?"

" I can meet you there at about nine."   To say that I felt euphoric was an understatement. I still had so many questions for him but I felt such a connection to him that I was sure he would have all the right answers for me. It took everything in me to not do a happy dance right there at work when we ended the call.

The rest of the day passed in a blur as I continued to work on Alaric's book. He had a great imagination and the way he made the characters come to life for me was brilliant. Before I knew it, everyone around me was gathering their things and getting ready to leave for the day. I looked at the clock and was a little shocked to realize so much time had passed.

I was on my way home, lost in my own thoughts, when the car behind me began flashing its headlights and following closely. Every horror movie I had ever seen began to flash before my eyes. This was a lonely stretch of road and I would be lucky to see another car before I reached home. If the car behind me was up to no good, I was in serious trouble.

I maneuvered my car into the other lane to let them pass, but they just got behind me again and continued doing the same thing. The road I was on was not very populated and although it was only five, it was already dark outside. The entire day had been dreary and gloomy.   I didn't want this car to follow me all the way home. I had no idea what the hell they wanted so I tried to pull off to the side to turn around but the second I slowed down, the car sped up and screeched around me. It was a silver blur as the tires kicked up loose gravel and smoked from braking so quickly. It had effectively blocked me in on the berm. I was trapped on the side of the road. I immediately felt a shiver of dread down my spine and my eyes were darting everywhere looking for a way out.

The car, which was none other than the silver Volvo with dark tinted windows, sat ominously still for just a moment while they had me boxed me in.   I had the ditch behind me and I had my car half turned and with their car in front, I had no recourse except to sit there and hope for some help. I briefly considered crashing into them to get them out of the way but that thought floated away like a fall leaf when I realized I might put myself in further danger if I tried that. I checked my cell phone and of course I didn't have a signal out this far. I knew I should have listened to Lindsey and gotten my concealed carry. My hands were sweating. I kept moving my cell phone in different directions hoping against all odds that I would suddenly pick up a signal, but no such luck. Panic was beginning to set in and seep through every pore in my body. I could get out of the car and run but there was nowhere to run to. I started searching through my purse for something, anything I could use as a weapon but there was nothing to be had except a hairbrush, my wallet, and a few useless odds and ends. I considered taking my keys out of the ignition and holding one through my fingers to use to stab if necessary but I wanted to keep my keys in there in case I had a chance to flee. My mind was racing for answers and a way out.

Abruptly, all four doors of the vehicle opened in sync and five burly looking men stood up. Every single one of them looked like they just walked out of an Arnold Schwarzenegger competition. I froze and held my arms up in front of me. Every joint and muscle in my body seemed to tense. All around me, there was a blue light so bright, it seemed blinding and all encompassing. It was like being in the middle of a lightning storm. The light was bright blue and crackled like lightning. I could feel all the hairs on my body standing at attention with the pure electricity in the air. The intensity of the light was pushing them back and blinding them. I was a statue watching the light surrounding the men, obscuring their features from me.

I was so focused on the strange illumination, that I failed to notice what was happening behind me. Before I could move an inch, Alaric was racing around the back of my car with another man whose features were obscured from me. He ordered me to move over so he could drive. His eyes were pleading and I was only vaguely aware of the other man getting into my back seat. On instinct, I moved out of his way and plopped myself onto the passenger's seat. I had no idea how he maneuvered my car out of there, but soon we were racing on the roadway away from the silver Volvo and my would-be attackers.

"Are you ok?" He asked while trying to focus on me and the road. His eyes were beseeching.

My only response was to sit there and stare at him, trying to make sense of the last five minutes of my life. *What the hell had just happened? What was happening now?*All these thoughts were permeating my brain but I could not seem to vocalize any of them.

He gently placed his hand on my arm and told me it was going to be ok as he moved the car like a Nascar driver. As soon as his hand made contact with me, I felt very calm. The breath that I hadn't realized I had been holding released out in a long exhale. My shoulders, that had become rigid, relaxed back and I melted into the seat. I knew in the back of my mind that none of this made sense, but I didn't care. Alaric said it was going to be ok and so it would be. I almost felt like I was drugged because somewhere in my subconscious I was scattered. These men came out of nowhere with unforeseen intentions and the man I really barely knew came to the rescue and was driving me to an unknown destination. My subconscious told me I should take my first opportunity to get out of there, but I felt a numb sort of calm at the same time. I briefly took medication for anxiety when my mom passed away and it felt like that. I could have all these crazy thoughts running through my head but the medication made me feel like it was ok and I was calm. I wasn't on that medication anymore and there were red flags that my mind was grasping to hold onto but they disappeared like a mist.

We drove east for about an hour. My mind began to conjure up different scenarios.   Perhaps this was some kind of set up or maybe I was having another psychotic break. Maybe I am still lying on the floor of my little home and the past month has just been some weird hallucination, and I am going to wake up to my somewhat boring but predictable life. I didn't say anything and neither did they as the car continued east and the trees passed with amazing speed. We all just sat in uncomfortable silence. I could feel Alaric's worried eyes on me but I was too exhausted from the whole experience to even acknowledge it or gaze back at him.

The car began slowing down as we approached a house with a gated entrance. It was one of those wrought iron gates with a keycode, the kind that you only see in the movies or when you are in Hollywood and you take the Tour of the Stars homes. Alaric punched in a code and the gate yawned in front of us, allowing us access. When we coasted down the long driveway and the house came into view, it seriously looked like a mansion out of a movie. I was sure that at any moment, I would see cameras and lights and the men in the car with me would smile as the director yelled, *cut.*

You could probably fit about a hundred of my little cottages inside this house. It had a magnificent porch with large pillars that reminded me of houses you see in movies like, *Gone with the Wind.* The gardens were lit up with solar lights that illuminated elaborately sculpted bushes and artfully arranged flowers.

Alaric turned off the car and again asked if I was ok. That was when the man in the back moved forward and I finally saw his face. He was the other man from my dream, the one that stares at me like he is dying of thirst and I carry with me the last glass of water on earth. They both had identical looks of concern on their faces as they waited for my answer. My answer? I began talking a mile a minute asking every question I could think of.

"Who were those men? What did they want? How did they know I was going to be on that road? What was the blue light? How did you and this other man know I was on the road? Where are we?" The questions just spilled from my lips like a machine gun spitting bullets with no reprieve.   I suddenly felt like I had gotten onto a roller coaster that was taking me places I wasn't sure I wanted to be.

Alaric took the lead. He looked at me with his intense blue eyes and placed his arm around my shoulder steering me toward the interior of the house. I didn't even remember getting out of the car. We slowly walked with the other man trailing us

"This is all going to be difficult for you to believe at first. My brother Xander and I have known about you for a long time." He motioned to the man behind us.

"We have been watching out for you for a while knowing that you would get your powers and that the Crissnas would come. You have powers that you can not even begin to imagine and we are here to help you. Everything will be explained and make sense soon enough, but we should get inside and let the family know that we are ok. "

At this point, I am realizing it is not me that is losing my mind, but them. *I have powers? Everything will be explained?* These really sound like bad lines from a B movie. As soon as we passed the threshold, I was immediately enveloped into a woman's arms.

"Are you ok Phoebe?" she asked with a worried look creasing her kind eyes.

"Yes, I think so. I am trying to make sense of everything."

Xander introduced her as their mom, Belle. She stood at about five foot three inches. She was slender and looked like she was in her early forties. She had the same eye color as Alaric with Xander's warm expression and demeanor. She stepped back, presumably, so I could have a moment to collect myself. I was feeling like this was all some sort of crazy dream at the moment. Things like this just didn't happen to me or to anyone really, except in science fiction movies.

Their dad's name was Steven and he stood off to the side looking worried but quiet. He was very tall with a shock of blonde hair. He was dressed in a suit and looked like he was ready for a day at the office. He had Xander's warm chocolate brown eyes and looked to be around the same age as his wife.

Their sister Alyssa, who was probably the prettiest woman I had ever seen, walked over and told me we were going to go and get some coffee in the kitchen and let the family talk. She was very petite with short brown hair, and a bubbly energetic attitude. She nearly bounced over to where I was and put her arm around me and steered me toward the kitchen.

This entire family looked like they had walked out of a fashion magazine. I felt not only overwhelmed by all that had happened, but completely frumpy in front of these supermodel-like people. We walked through the massive house together in silence.

The house was beautiful with polished hardwood floors and high, vaulted ceilings. There were oil paintings hung on nearly every wall and I had no doubt they were very expensive originals. There were beautiful area rugs strewn intricately throughout each room we walked through . It seemed like we had walked a mile through the house by the time we reached the kitchen.

When we arrived there, it was unlike any kitchen I had ever seen. Even Gordon Ramsay would have been envious. It was impossible to even tell where the appliances were because everything was covered with polished wood. The cupboards were very impressive and looked like they cost more than my entire cottage. I didn't realize where the refrigerator was until she moved a wooden panel and behind it was a massive stainless steel refrigerator. She pulled out some creamer and then grabbed some sugar from the cupboard next to the refrigerator. She offered me some coffee and I happily accepted. I had a seat on the bench at the island in the middle of the kitchen as she poured me some coffee.

"So, tell me all about what happened. I want every detail. I hope the boys didn't scare you."

I don't know why I opened up to her. I felt like she was trustworthy and her demeanor put me at ease. I told her about the five guys on the road. She asked if the "boys' had explained about the Crissnas? When I said no she asked if they had explained anything. That is when I think I finally broke.

"I have no idea what is going on. For years I kept dreaming of those two "boys" as you call them. I then ran into Alaric a few weeks ago and then again yesterday. Then, I was driving home minding my own business when these men had me and my car cornered, a bright blue light flashed, and out of the darkness came Alaric and Xander. All of this just seems so surreal. There is no way a book editor from nowhere Ohio suddenly has people following her, two men from her dream suddenly real and in her life, and now some group called the Crissnas are after me? That sounds like the name of a rock band, by the way." I said all of this in what I was sure was a dramatic fashion. I know I was talking faster than the speed of light and I briefly wondered if she could even comprehend what I was saying. I didn't think I could handle too much more. The thought of having a complete mental breakdown in this opulent space was not out of the question.

Alyssa must have sensed my distress and unease. She walked around the island, moved our cups out of the way, and hugged me tightly. I just sat there a minute, completely unaccustomed to a stranger hugging me, and then gave in and placed my arms around her shoulders. I needed someone to understand what I was going through. I needed my mom. She was always the voice of reason in my life and whenever I found myself in some trouble, I always tried to imagine what she would say. Trying to concentrate on that now, I really could not fathom what kind of advice my mom would give me for this one.

"What do you know about your mom and her family?" she asked as she backed up and sat back down. *Could she somehow know that I had just been thinking about my mom?*

I was pretty confused by her question. " I lost my mom a few years ago and I never met any of her family. She always told me that she was never close with any of them and they were better off out of our lives. My dad grew up in an orphanage so I don't know any more about his side of the family than he did. He has not really been a part of my life ever since my mom passed."

"Ok, Phoebe. This is all going to be a lot to take in but I need you to just listen. Your mom was a part of our race. We are technically vampires but not the kind you have read about in any books or have seen on late-night horror movies. Our people can be out in the sunlight, it doesn't affect us. We are born just like humans. We don't bite people to turn them into one of us. It doesn't work that way." She paused for a moment, looked at me perhaps to gauge my acceptance. Whatever she saw on my face must have given her encouragement because she continued with her outlandish story.

"We eat food just like any human does or we can drink blood, we can survive on either or a combination of both. Blood gives our race a certain advantage but it isn't a necessity. We have certain abilities, unlike humans, and we do have eternal life. Once we reach a certain age, we can stop or slow the aging process. We can die if we are separated from our kind for a very long time though. We begin to lose our abilities and become almost human. That is why your mom was able to pass, because she stayed away. "

I stopped her at that point. "Wait, but if what you are saying is true and I am a Vampire, then my mom was around another Vampire so she should not have passed away, right?" This was all too bizarre and what she just stated was really contradictory.

"You had not come into your powers yet, so just being in your presence was not enough to keep your mom from getting ill. "

Well, that just made me feel all shades of awful like it was my fault that my mom got sick in the first place and why I would never see her again. She must have picked up on what I was thinking because her next words were like a soothing balm.

"Your mom made a choice, Phoebe. She knew what she was doing and wanted to live an ordinary human life with a beginning and a clear end. She never wanted everything that came with this life. She didn't want you anywhere near the Crissnas. Her greatest wish was to give you as normal of a childhood as possible, and she did that. She made those choices out of love, so please don't try to carry that weight of that on your shoulders. It is what she wanted."

She took a brief break from her explanations to squeeze my hand and assure herself that I was ok before going on.

"Your dad is the man who raised you but he is not your true father. We are not exactly sure who your real dad is but we know he is one of us."

"With our kind, once we reach adolescence, we begin to get our abilities and we also begin to dream about our soul mate. That is our way of preparing us for what is to come in this life. You probably didn't get any of your abilities right away because you were separated from us."

I am certain that I was sitting there with my mouth open. I began to stand up and back away from the island slowly. I understood now. These people were delusional. There is no way she could believe what she just told me unless she is either crazy or high. She didn't make any move to get up which gave me a little piece of mind. When I reached the door, I stopped moving from the kitchen and turned to her. I don't know what made me stop, as any sane person would be running away as fast as possible. Maybe I wasn't very sane.

"Let me get this straight, I am a vampire. My mom was a vampire and whoever my real dad is or was is also a vampire? I have abilities I don't know about and I am dreaming of my soul mate?   Then, why am I dreaming of Alaric and Xander? I knew them before I met them from my dreams about them. My mom definitely would have told me if I had abilities and was some creature of the night, no offense. This is all a little too much. And who are the Crissnas? Are they some vampire hunting group?"

"The Crissnas are also vampires but they are more like the kind that you have read about in books. Their group is not born, but made by a bite from another of their kind. They can't be in the sunlight and they do drink blood to stay alive. They have been trying to eradicate our race for as long as we have existed. They don't like that we have inherent abilities and that we live as we do and they are limited."

She took a breath, and realizing I wasn't trying to escape she continued on.

"We first learned about you about six years ago. Alaric began having dreams about you and we found you and your mom. She was just beginning to become ill and she asked that once the time came that she could no longer protect you ,that we protect you. Then, Xander began having dreams. That is the part we still haven't figured out."

At this point, the whole family walked into the kitchen and Alyssa halted our conversation. Steven and his wife sat down, while Alaric and Xander stood across the room looking worried. Steven suggested that I stay with them to ensure my safety since the Crissnas were starting to come after me.

" I couldn't possibly. This is all just too much for me right now." I still wasn't entirely sure they weren't all insane and in any case I needed some time to process everything that I had seen and heard in the past few hours.

"We will take shifts watching over you until the danger passes. Usually, the Crissnas will give up once they realize we are rallied together. Your mom asked us to look after you and we take that obligation very seriously."

I agreed and he said Alaric would drive me home and take the first shift. I thanked them all and walked out with Alaric once he grabbed some of his things. The family hung back at the door looking worried as we ventured to the car.

Once I got in the car with him, it felt like my whole body was tingling. I had never had these types of feelings for anyone before. Yes, I had boyfriends before, but I never felt like this. It was indescribable. In his presence, I felt calm even though the world was going crazy around me. I felt like I wanted to grab onto him and never let go, but I held myself in check. This entire situation was like something out of a crazy novel that I am supposed to be editing. Not one thing made any sense and it could not be real. I could not be a vampire and have feelings for another vampire that I only technically met once before. I was not the dramatic type of person, nor was I the type who thought she was in love with someone she didn't know well. I had never been in love in my life and I was sure this was nothing more than a serious case of lust. Even with everything that had happened tonight, I still wanted to rip his clothes off and have my way with him. Once I felt like I could form an intelligent sentence, I asked him to tell me whatever he could about all of this. He said he heard what Alyssa told me.

"Our kind has always existed and co-existed with humans. Each one of us has different abilities that usually begin to manifest in adolescence. I can feel what others are feeling, sort of like an empath."

At that point, I am pretty sure my entire body went up in flames. I could feel my cheeks burning and I was thankful for the dark so he couldn't see how embarrassed I was. *He can feel what others are feeling*? Oh shit! That is not going to be good! At least he couldn't read my mind. The things he would have seen. Ok, my face was definitely bright red by now.

" I was wondering if you could tell me where the blue light came from tonight? Was that some sort of trick that you or Xander can do or did you have some sort of technology that I don't know about?"

At this point, he took a deep breath, looked at me and pulled the car over to the side of the road. Ok, this must be the point when he is supposed to kill me and get rid of the evidence. I moved my body as far toward the door as I could, getting ready to make a break for it if I needed to. He seemed to notice my discomfort so he gently took my hands in his and waited for a moment for me to calm down. He had that kind of effect on me and soon I was serene enough to see what was going to happen next. He still held my left hand in his warm hands and stared into my eyes with his piercing stare until he was ready to speak or until he thought I was ready to listen.

"Phoebe, that light came from you. We didn't do that, you did." He then paused and looked at me to gauge how I was going to take that news. If I was being completely honest with myself, I felt that it was coming from me and somewhere in the back of my mind I knew that but I was unwilling to admit it until now. Maybe this whole thing was real and they all weren't crazy. Vampires are real and I am one of them. It felt a bit like the wall I had built arpound myself since this night began started to crumble a bit.

"Honestly, it looked to me like it was holding them back and burning them a bit. I couldn't feel much of what they were feeling because of the light so that also blocked my power. I have never seen one of us do something like that before. I was very impressed! Do you know of any other powers you have?"

I started to say no but then I thought back to when I was kissing him on the dance floor and I could see images of myself through his eyes. *How was I supposed to bring that up?* Maybe that was a conversation for another time so I told him I didn't know of any other abilities.

He told me that I would find out with time. Usually we have one ability that is all our own but others that we all have. Those are abilities such as speed, intensified senses, and of course immortality.

"We just need to be careful at night because of the Crissnas. That is when my family and I will watch over you from now on. Once you head off to work in the morning, I will go home and talk with them to try to figure some of this out." He seemed so calm and kind. He spoke in a way that was both soothing and also kept my senses alert because he was so alluring to me. He was a sea of calm and gentle waves that made me want to jump right into the surf.

The conversation with his sister kept creeping back into my mind, especially the part about the soul mate. First of all, I never really believed in soul mates to begin with. *Secondly, how can one have two soul mates? Why would I be dreaming of them both?* That makes absolutely no sense and I wanted to talk to Alaric about it but considering how I barely knew him and how I was feeling so lustful toward him, I figured that too should be a conversation for another time. He started the car back in the direction of my house and we sat silently for the rest of the ride there. I needed time to process all of this and I was tired of talking and hearing things I was not ready to hear.

We arrived at my house with no directions from me so obviously he had been watching me for a while. Again, he walked around to my side of the car to let me out in a fraction of a second. That is something I would never get used to. Speed is obviously one of his traits. I wondered if I would get to be that fast as well. As I exited the car, the cool breeze caressed my skin and allowed me to clear my head. He stood next to me for a moment just gazing at me with an unreadable expression . I wondered what was going through his mind. His hair was being tousled by the wind as if it too wanted to reach out and touch it, to feel if it was as sleek as it seemed. I envied the wind as we strolled slowly into my house.

I turned on the lights illuminating the cozy but very homey place I call home. I loved every inch of this place. It was made for comfort and relaxation and that is what I craved after a long day at work. The kitchen was the first room we walked into. It was a little space with all the normal appliances and a cute little table for two in the middle that I always adorned with fresh flowers. On the counter next to my coffee maker was my diffuser. I loved to put the scent of blueberry in that one to mimic the smell of blueberry muffins baking in the oven. I offered him something to drink. I handed him a bottle of water from the fridge and our fingers brushed as he took it. It was like a jolt of electricity to my senses. I was hyper aware of his fingers brushing mine, the look of pleasure on his face, and his muscles straining against the thin fabric of his shirt. I needed to do something to distract myself before I made a fool out of myself like I believed I did at the club all those weeks ago.

I excused myself and walked to the closet in the hallway near the living room. This room was also on the small side but it was peaceful with its warm beige walls, scent diffuser with the butterscotch scent on the little wooden table, couch that allowed a person to sink into and relax, and a cozy little fireplace. After a long day at work, it was the perfect place to decompress. I grabbed some blankets for him to camp out on the couch. I wanted to invite him to camp out in my bed, but decided to at least try to have a little self- control. Our hands touched when I handed him the blankets and it was like a fire ignited inside of me. He looked at me with an intensity that was making my bones turn to jelly. All of the sudden, I saw this rush of images. Images of him growing up. Images of his parents, his little sister, and Xander as children running around and chasing each other. Then, an image of me on the dance floor with him kissing him and the feeling of completeness. He saw me as this beautiful mysterious woman. I could feel what he was feeling when he kissed me for the first time. He was absolutely awed that I wanted him too. I let my fingers drop away from his hand like I had touched a hot stove. This was all too much for one night. This entire scenario of me being anything other than human and possessing crazy powers was just too overwhelming and there were moments I knew it was true in my heart and others that I figured we were all material fit for the looney bin.

"I'm sorry Alaric. I just....this is just a lot to take in. It's not that I don't want...well you know. I just need to.."

"It's ok Phoebe. I know. I understand. There is going to be plenty of time for us to talk about this, all of this, and us."

With that, I turned around to get to my room. I could feel his gaze following me but I knew if I looked back, I would lose my resolve. My room was on the small side with a queen bed and a small dresser and closet. It was big enough for me and my bed was so soft and comfortable so I didn't mind the size of the room so much. I walked over to my bed and flopped onto it. I was worn out from everything and I needed some serious sleep. I covered up with my soft blankets and curled up on my side. I tried to relax and let myself drift off to sleep, but I couldn't shut off my brain. *I have powers and two men that have feelings for me. I am a vampire and my mom was too.* The part about my dad not being my dad completely made sense now. He must have known I wasn't his, so he never really cared. A real man wouldn't have minded if I was really his. A real man would have loved me anyway. Alaric was on my couch and all I wanted to do was go out there and jump on him. He just exudes sexiness. He is like a walking advertisement for sex. *How am I ever going to sleep? Did I hurt those guys with my blue light? My blue light, that came from me!?!* It was exciting and crazy all at the same time. I, ordinary book editor Phoebe, had powers. I could stop five grown men from coming after me. Wow! *Who was my real dad? Did he know about me?* Those were my last thoughts as I drifted off sleep.

Chapter Five

The New Reality

I must have fallen asleep at some point because there I was in the same dream I had been having. I was once again running through the forest but this time I didn't feel as scared. I felt as though my running was effortless, even though I was going just as fast as I had before. I knew what lay up ahead. I knew they were there just waiting for me and I was certain I would make it. I got to the clearing as the Crissnas slunk back into the shadows behind me. This time, Alaric and Xander both took a few steps toward me. I outstretched my hands and felt so safe and loved and then I woke up. I still couldn't figure out who I chose. It was so frustrating to wake up before the good part!

It was time to get ready for work anyway. I went into the bathroom to get ready before Alaric could see what a mess I was in the morning and decided to go screaming in the other direction. After a nice warm shower, I put on my work clothes, some light makeup and straightened my hair. After one last look in the mirror, I realized starting my day could not be put off any longer.

When I sauntered into the living room, the blankets were folded up on the couch and he had eggs and cinnamon rolls ready for me in the kitchen. He is sexy, he cooks, and is possibly my soul mate. I had no words for how amazing that sounded in my head. He looked up as I entered the kitchen. He still looked a bit drowsy, and I couldn't help but wonder if our proximity had bothered him as well last night.

"Did you sleep ok Phoebe?"

" I tried, but too many things were going through my mind. Thanks for making breakfast. You really didn't have to." I said as I grabbed a cinnamon roll and some juice. I perched myself in the chair but could not tear my eyes away while I nibbled on my cinnamon roll.

"It's ok. I wanted to. Xander will be here in a few minutes to pick me up. We are all going to have a strategy meeting to try to figure all of this out today. One of us will follow you home from work and keep you safe tonight."

Just as he said that we heard a car pull up out front. After a peek out the window, he walked over and gave me a kiss on the forehead and said he would see me soon. His eyes burned with what he really wanted to do. He placed his forehead against mine and held lightly to my shoulders. It was intense but oddly comforting. He took a deep breath and let go. He walked out the door but his scent lingered in my kitchen. It was a heady scent of sandalwood and sunshine mixed with the eggs and cinnamon rolls still sitting on my table.

It took me a few minutes to get out of my head. It was difficult not to ponder on the last twenty four hours. Before my anxiety got out of control, I ate a little, tidied up, and went to work.

No matter what I did, I could not concentrate on my tasks, which was a first for me. I kept reading the same page over and over and never really digesting any of it. I needed to look at the facts objectively, without any of my emotions taking control of my internal conversation. The first truth was that I had been dreaming about Alaric and Xander since I was sixteen. I had never met them before all of this craziness started happening so it wasn't like I knew them and then manifested them into a dream.

So, the dream was unexplainable. Three weeks ago, I ran into Alaric and had a very hot makeout session with him, where I began to see images of myself at various stages of my life. Maybe that part was something I was thinking of all on my own, even though that really didn't seem plausible. Then, I got chased by five men and allegedly rescued by Alaric and Xander and their entire family told me I have powers, and we are all Vampires. Not to forget, the Crissnas, who are also Vampires, but the dangerous kind, are after me. Those last parts are their truths, I still wasn't sure they were not out of their minds.

I really was trying to tackle this from a logical and scientific angle. They could all be having a mass delusion, they could all be in on some plot against me, but to what end? Things like this just didn't happen outside of books. Vampires were not real! Next thing you know, they are going to expect me to believe that all mythical creatures are real. There was my growing desire for Alaric, that was definitely real. But how could I allow myself to be so attracted to him if he was crazy or working against me? Without any realistic explanations for everything that had been occurring, I decided that the best course of action was to just allow them to think that I believed them and see what would happen next. Honestly, in some moments I did believe it all and others I doubted everything. I didn't get the feeling that any of them were a real threat to me. To be honest, I really couldn't picture myself cutting Alaric off, if anything else. I needed to see what this was truly about and if they were all maniacal. I wanted desperately for this to somehow be true because I really felt such a strong pull toward Alaric and I had never felt that before for anyone.

In what seemed like no time at all, it was time for me to go home. I didn't get any work accomplished today which left me feeling guilty and a little stressed. I started to wonder who was going to be waiting to follow me home. *Would it be Alaric again? Would I be able to keep my hands to myself if it was?* I soon found out the answer to that when I heard a tap on my cubicle wall as I was gathering my things to leave. There stood Xander, and I was immediately relaxed. Until that moment, I hadn't realized how tense my muscles had been all day. I was going to need to book a massage once all this was figured out. I had some aches and pains where I wasn't even sure I had muscles.

Being around Xander felt like home, which truthfully didn't make one ounce of sense since I hardly knew him. His mere presence made me feel calm and relaxed. Maybe that was his power and perhaps everyone felt that way around him.

He was wearing khakis and a button down shirt. His normally artfully arranged hair was tousled like he had recently gotten out of bed. If it weren't for my strong attraction to Alaric, I might be more tempted by him. He just stood there with his hand outstretched to me sort of like he was in my dream last night. I felt like if I blinked my eyes he would vanish. I took his hand and we walked out in silence and it just felt right.

"Is it ok if we just drive your car? I had Alyssa drop me off. I figured it was safer if we were both in the same vehicle."

"Of course. How is Alyssa and everyone else?"

"They are doing well, although a bit frazzled trying to piece together what we know about you and the Crissnas. We are just trying to figure out more about your ability with the blue light and how we can best protect you. We have never seen powers like yours before. Usually our abilities have something to do with the mind. We can see things or do things but it doesn't often manifest itself so physically like your blue light did."

"Oh. I had no idea. Nothing is wrong with me, right?"

"It's funny. I tell you that we have never seen powers like yours and instead of worrying that you have abilities, you ask if something is wrong because yours are different." He said this with a smile on his beautiful face. He really should smile more often but he seems to be the quiet and serious type, the total opposite of Alaric. When he smiles, it is like someone turned on the light in a room that has never seen the light of day before.

I kind of chuckled. It sounded a little crazy. We got a few curious looks from co-workers as we walked to my car. I had quite a few acquaintances at work but no real friends so I wasn't worried about whatever impression I may or may not be making by walking to my car with Xander. I did have to wonder though what they were thinking. The other day I left with Alaric and today I am leaving with Xander and I never even give any of the men I work with a chance.

As I drove us to the house we made idle conversation about how our day was. He was easy to talk to and be with. It felt like I had known him my entire life. I kept catching him out of the corner of my eye staring at me when we weren't talking. He really was amazing to be around but I didn't get the feelings that I got when I was with Alaric.

When we got home, he did a sweep of the perimeter and the house before he would let me get out of the car. I felt a little impatient, I wasn't used to anyone looking out for me. I had always taken care of myself so this entire situation was difficult to deal with because I had to give up a certain amount of control and I wasn't entirely secure doing that. When he gave the all clear, we went in and it occurred to me that I hadn't really been shopping for food for a bit. It was kind of hard to cook for just one person so I ate out a lot. I opened the fridge and I had some wine, eggs, and some left- over salad along with this morning's cinnamon rolls. I suggested we run back out and pick something up. He suggested we go out to dinner to get to know each other better. I was intrigued by the idea. After all, he was one of two people I had been dreaming about and I would like to know what was behind that serene and serious facade.

I told him to give me a few minutes to freshen up. I changed into a black dress, brushed my teeth, and freshened up my makeup. When I walked back into the living room he just kind of stared for a moment. I began to wonder if I had forgotten something or maybe I sprouted two heads. I couldn't decipher his expression and it made me a little uneasy. I began to fidget, wondering if I should suggest we should leave or if I should go back in front of the mirror to see what was wrong.

Before I had the chance to think about this too much, he walked over and took my hand. He kissed the back of it and said, "You look absolutely stunning. " He then got a shy smile on his face and looked down as we began silently walking to the door. He and Alaric were so different. With Alaric I feel like my whole body is on fire and I can't get enough of him. He is just so sexy. With Xander, it just feels right like this is where I am supposed to be. He is home somehow. I think we both just have that introverted vibe, like we are kindred spirits. We talked a little about his abilities on the way to the restaurant. Xander has the ability to heal others with his touch. Somehow this seems very fitting for him and his calm personality. I really do want to believe that all of this is possible.

He really is very attractive. He has a strong square jaw, penetrating brown eyes, and thick brown hair. We made it to the restaurant and being the gentleman that he is, he walked around and opened the car door for me and led me into the restaurant by placing his hand on the small of my back. It was very comforting and nice. He chose a little out of the way Italian Restaurant. It was very cozy and charming inside and the people were very welcoming. It was just as expensive as the Chinese Restaurant where Alaric took me but the atmosphere was very different. It was open and airy with a lot of light and boisterous decor. The waiters were dressed in lively red outfits and crisp white aprons.

We were soon seated over in the corner far away from the door. We were close to the kitchen and the most amazing aroma was wafting from that direction. As we were ordering our food, the waitress couldn't seem to keep her eyes off of Xander. It was actually pretty irritating but he didn't even seem to notice her attention. At least that part of the evening very much reminded me of my date with Alaric. I must not be the only female that finds them fascinating.

"So, tell me about your work. It must be very interesting to be able to go through and edit books and enter a new universe every day."

"That is a nice way of looking at it. I am able to tune out everything and everyone when I am reading and editing. I have always been able to do that when I read. It is like entering a new and different world each time I pick up a new book. I found your brother's book to be the most intriguing I have read in a long time. I had never considered the topic before and now it seems I am immersed in it outside of the book as well." I got quiet while the waitress brought over our salads.

"It sounds like a fun career. I understand you are also writing your own book. I am sure it will be wonderful. I would love to read it when you are ready. I love to read anything and everything I possibly can." He paused for a moment. "I went to college this most recent time to become a veterinarian."

I could picture him in a room with a bunch of dogs and cats. Then, I realized he said, this past time. "How many times have you been to college?"

"Oh, you caught that." If he were capable of blushing, I am sure he would be right now. He looked down for a moment. "I have been quite a few times. I have tried out different careers. I don't like to sit around and get bored. Eternity is a long time so I like to try new things. I have particularly enjoyed being a veterinarian though. I really enjoy being around animals, they don't judge or stare. People, humans, seem to have a sense that we are different. They have varied reactions to us but mostly they stare and it gets a little annoying. I just want to enjoy my time here, with the people I care about, and not have to endure the prying eyes of people I don't know. I haven't been working for a few months because Alaric and I have been splitting up the duty of watching over you for a while because we could sense the Crissnas closing in. Keeping you safe is my priority now."

Suddenly, I was drowning in guilt, I didn't want to be the reason he had to leave a career he loved, even if it was temporary. It was my fault he had to watch over me, my stomach felt hollowed out and my head was buzzing with remorse. None of this was fair at all. If mom had just told me who I really was, maybe all of this would be different. She had to have had her reasons, I just wish she were still around so I could ask her what those reasons were. I wish I could ask her why she married my dad, especially considering he isn't my real dad. I wanted to ask her who my real dad is and why she didn't end up with him. I will never get the chance to ask any of this and that is more frustrating than I can put into words. There was this entire whole world I knew nothing about. It was unreal. Time for me to stop being a baby and wondering and worrying. It was time for me to start finding answers to my questions instead of expecting everyone else to take care of me and my safety. It wasn't fair for Xander, Alaric, or any of their family to have to stop their lives to take care of me, someone they barely know.

I stopped my inner monologue to let out a little gasp. I really was beginning to believe that all of this is true. I don't know what made me turn that corner, but there I was. The thought of it left me a little in awe, like when you watch a car wreck or even a baby being born. It is a bit surreal and seems to happen in slow motion. I am not sure yet if my new reality will be more like a new chance or a car wreck waiting to steal my life away.

"Can we go to your house after dinner? I need to get some answers and I need to learn how to start watching my own back instead of expecting everyone else to do it for me."

He nodded his assent as his eyes gave away his silent approval of my request. Just then, the waitress came with the most delicious smelling food, it took both of our minds off of the previous conversation. We ate a delicious cheese ravioli and talked about the weather, college, and careers. I think we both silently agreed to keep the heavy conversation for later. I learned that Xander was a lot like me. He craved the simple life with the few family and friends that are meaningful. He has a nurturing side which shows in everything he says and does. He seems like the type that would choose to sit at home and have a date night where he cooked dinner and he and his date relaxed in front of a fire. That was a lot like me, but I also had an adventurous side, where I wanted to travel and explore either on my own or with someone special. That was the part of me that was very attracted to Alaric because he seems like the bold type and I needed something and someone like that in my life. I need to be challenged to get out of my comfort zone and Alaric could be the one to do that.

Chapter Six

Answers

We left the restaurant and I had so many questions swirling through my mind on the way to his house, I was quiet. Xander was very intuitive, he allowed me to sit and ponder everything that was happening without expecting me to make conversation. I assumed he could sense my resolve to get to the bottom of all of this.

We arrived at his beautiful home. I wondered if I would ever get used to its grandeur or if I would always be struck speechless and its beauty and magnificent size. His family was waiting for us and it seemed that they were prepared for all of my questions. Anyway, they were all seated in the living room and when we walked in their attention was solely focused on me. It made me a little uncomfortable but even more determined to get to the bottom of this and protect myself.

Alyssa was sitting in the fluffiest chair I had ever seen, her body seemed to be swallowed by it. She still had that same bubbly energy that I remembered from when I met her. She seemed like she could spring out of the chair at any moment, her life force was something so tangible, you could almost see the aura surrounding her.

His mom and dad were seated next to each other on the couch, holding hands, looking like they were ready for anything. They were what I had always wished my parents could have been. I never saw my parents holding hands or looking totally relaxed with each other and in tune. It must have been wonderful to grow up with parents that were so caring about their family and each other.

Alaric was sitting on a chair big enough for two and stood up, took my hand and sat with me. Xander stood for a moment and for a fraction of a second, had a fleeting look like he wanted to stick a pin on the seat under Alaric. As soon as I saw the expression, it faded and with a resolved sigh, he finally sat next to his parents.

"First of all, this is not fair that all of your lives have had to come to a screeching halt because I needed protection, so that needs to end now. I am a grown up and a vampire with powers presumably. I need to figure out how to use them to defend myself so everyone can go back to their lives. " I stated all of this in my most determined voice letting them know I would not take no for an answer. I gazed at each of their faces. Each one showing a different reaction. Alaric and Xander both beamed with pride, Alyssa looked like she was trying to stifle a giggle, and Steven and Belle looked even more concerned.

They protested of course but I wouldn't hear of it. " I am starting to accept what I am and I will deal with that. I just need a way to figure out what my powers are so that I can use them to protect myself."

They suggested we go out back so I could try my blue light in the backyard where I couldn't hurt anyone. When I walked into their backyard it was almost like being in the forest in my dream. It was so secluded and peaceful. I could hear wildlife scurrying in the trees. The sun was just beginning its descent in the sky and it cast an ethereal look to the surroundings. Beams of light filtered through the trees and I had a sudden urge to run through the foliage and find a secluded place to sit down and collect my thoughts, but there was no time for that.

"Try to hit the log over there with your light." Alaric suggested. He looked at me like he believed I would have no problem doing as he requested. I looked at him and there was doubt in my eyes, I was still trying to convince myself that this world was real and I was a part of it. I cast my eyes away from him and to the log that he indicated. I attempted to picture myself throwing the light at the log.

I concentrated and I tried, but nothing happened. He walked over so quickly that he was a blur and it startled me. He placed his hand gently on my shoulder and told me to just relax. I looked at his face to see that he had this air of confidence in me that I just didn't feel. I took a deep breath, closed my eyes for a moment breathing in his scent of sandalwood and sunshine and opened my eyes to try again. That time when I tried, I was able to project the blue light onto the log. That is when we all realized, it wasn't just blue light, it was a sort of blue fire. It lit up the log with its blue blazing splendor and we were all a bit astonished until Alyssa threw her arm up and the fire miraculously went out. I guess I could figure out one of her talents.

I had resolved myself to believe that everything they were telling me was true but until that moment, I hadn't truly accepted it. Now, I had no other choice. I had just set a log on fire with blue electricity that pulsed from my fingertips.

They told me to try again with a fallen log about one hundred feet away and I was able to replicate what I had done to the other log. Immediately, Alyssa put out the fire for me. Again, and again I was able to hit targets no matter how close or how far away. Every time I did this, it was like all of my nerve endings were alive and lit up like lightning that sparked the sky during a storm. Well, at least I could protect myself.

"How can I figure out what other hidden talents I have?" I directed that question to Steven.

"You are going to have to be patient and wait until they present themselves to you. These were all highly unusual circumstances. This is the first time a vampire of our kind has been separated from birth, therefore nothing is going to be the way it usually is." Steven was so much like Xander it was uncanny. He was so calm and seemed so wise.

Suddenly, I had a vision of the burly guys from last night creeping up on their home. I started to warn them but Alaric yelled to everyone that the Crissnas had somehow breached the gate and were headed for us. We all went into defense mode. Let's just say that with all of them standing there, they made a formidable force to recon with. If I weren't standing with them as an ally, I would be very frightened.

The Crissnas soon crept around the corner and I immediately hit them with a blast of blue fire and Alyssa hit them with a blast of wind. The rest of the family began running toward them ready for a fight. They were still trying to put out their clothes which had caught on fire. They were beating at the flames and rolling around. All of them stared in fright at the family that was coming straight at them. It was like a synchronized dance, Steven and Belle were at the forefront gracefully eating up the space between them and the Crissnas. Alyssa, Alaric, and Xander fanned out in a pattern behind their parents ready to engage the enemy. I stood off to the side, and began to raise my arms again in their direction. They all shared terrified looks and then began to run in the opposite direction. They had all managed to beat out the flames from their clothes but were left with partially charred pants and shirts that were in tatters. Once they were off of the property and long gone, everyone retreated back inside. I felt like I was at the bottom of a roller coaster that had just plummeted from a great height and was about to go up again at any moment. My senses were heightened and I felt on edge waiting for the next shoe to drop.

Xander asked, "How did you know they were coming?" The entire family had taken their seats in the family room again and none of them looked like they had even broken a sweat dealing with those guys. They all had their eyes on Alaric, waiting for his answer.

"Don't look at me! I just told you what Phoebe projected to me." He said with a sly know-it-all grin. I was hoping that he would not place the spotlight on me again and I gave him an aggravated look, as he continued to smirked at me.

" I just saw them in my mind creeping around the front of the house and then there they were. I really don't know how I did it. Another ability?" I realize at this point, there should be some panic button being pushed in my brain, but I was really more interested in their reaction and a little stoked about what might happen next. Every kid dreams of growing up to be Superman or Wonder Woman, and here I was with real powers. I was able to help this family defeat an enemy that had the intention of harming everyone here. That was pretty amazing in my book.

Xander then turned to Alaric with a look somewhere between disbelief and discouragement. This is when Alaric looked at me with that sexy lopsided grin I was growing accustomed to and reiterated that I projected what I saw into his mind.

At this point, everyone except Alaric stared at me like they had never seen me before. I didn't know if I should feel proud or scared as hell. Xander looked like he was ready to go back and look for those Crissnas and rip them to shreds. All of their faces had identical looks of shock except for Alaric's which looked like he had just won the lottery. It seemed like time was suspended and no one spoke. I didn't know what to do as I stood there feeling very unsure of myself and began worrying at the hem on my shirt.

Belle was the first to speak. "Only soul mates who have been together for years are able to do that and sometimes even then they never reach that point." She spoke in the most soothing voice, presumably because she knew I was concerned and would be even more upset once what she had stated processed in my frizzled brain.

It was my turn to look stunned and stare at everyone. The only person who seemed very pleased with himself was Alaric. He was still standing there staring at me in a way that made me want to just run up and devour him in front of everyone. His smile kicked up a notch which had me wondering if he could read those thoughts too. Belle, Steven, and Alyssa seemed guarded ready to respond to whatever happened. Xander looked like he might have steam coming from his ears. His face was red and his nose was flaring as if he was a dragon ready to breathe fire.

"So far, Phoebe has shown us three talents. She can throw blue fire. She can see what is happening in her mind just before it happens, and she can project her thoughts to Alaric. Phoebe, try to think of something and project your thoughts to one of us, other than Alaric." Steven suggested.

I kept thinking of a song I had stuck in my head, "A Thousand Years," and tried projecting that to Steven. I stared at him while I thought of the lyrics and he just shook his head indicating he couldn't hear my thoughts. I tried each one of them in turn and the only one it worked with was Alaric.

Xander looked at the floor, defeated. "I waited my entire life for you and the only connection you seem to have is to Alaric. I don't understand. I started having dreams about you long ago and you hold my heart in your hands. I am yours. Why can't you be mine?"

I felt like someone had just dropped an atomic bomb on me. I was shaken to the core. I didn't feel that way for Xander. The way he was wilting before my eyes made the guilt eat me up inside. I was sure I was going to be sick.

I felt something for him, but not that. How could he feel that way for me already when he hardly knew me?

"Xander, we don't know anything for sure. I just met both of you. Yes, I understand that we are all having these dreams about each other and that has to mean something. I just found out who I really am and that my life has really been a complete lie. I haven't even begun to process any of this. I like you Xander, but this is a lot to lay at my feet right now." I sagged back in the chair feeling completely deflated. "We don't know that for sure."

"We don't know what for sure Phoebe?" Steven asked.

" I was just answering Alaric." I stated. Everyone looked between Alaric and I like something was going on that I was oblivious to. Alaric just sat back and took it all in.

Steven said, "Alaric didn't say anything."

"Yes, he said that we are soul mates." I wasn't even sure I believed in soul mates. It wasn't like I had much success with men. I had been on my share of dates but I always found some kind of fault with every single one of them. They were either too boring or too crazy. Some of them seemed like they just wanted a fun time and others seemed like they wanted a relationship. My longest relationship lasted about a week. I just wasn't that interested in any of them. I figured I would end up to be the old cat lady that everyone pitied. It didn't really bother me until now. Now, it seemed like I had two guys who, by the way, I barely knew and had no idea if I had anything other than my species in common with either of them, wanting to be with me.

Alaric said, "Phoebe, I was thinking that. I never said anything out loud."

Everyone looked at me to see my reaction. I sat with my mouth slightly parted, contemplating what this new ability was supposed to mean. "Never mind," I said. "I think I should head home. I am coming to terms with this but I really need some alone time to get a grasp on all of it. Plus, I have to be at work early tomorrow."

"I will drive you home and keep watch tonight," Xander told me. I did my best to protest because it was obvious that I could fight back with my blue fire but everyone seemed to be in agreement that it was their job to look out for me. I stopped protesting and just allowed him to drive me home.

The ride home was spent in silence. I felt too tight in my own skin thinking about what Xander had just professed to me back there. I was thinking about everything that had happened to me in the span of just a few short days and I tried not to think about what he might be thinking or feeling at that moment. When we got to my house, he checked everything out before I could go in. I got out the blankets for him to sleep on the couch and he looked at me like he really wanted me to remember something or wanted to tell me something but he simply thanked me for the blankets. I went to my room, and we both went to sleep. That night there was no tossing and turning. I was exhausted from everything that had happened and was emotionally spent, so I slept like a baby.

The next morning when I got up for work, Xander was gone. He left a note that someone would be there after work to get me. I thought it seemed out of character for him to just leave without a word but I really didn't know him well enough to make that assumption. I grabbed some coffee and went to work again, immersing myself in other people's books. It was a very nice and needed escape from my own unraveling life. This time I left my mind blank and allowed the words of the book to flow through me like a river, carrying me with the current to a better place.

I finished reading Alaric's book and I really let all of the information soak in. *Was he writing about a situation that had really happened? Was he writing about me?* There were a lot of parallels between me and the main heroine of his novel. We had both lost our mother and didn't know who our real father was. We both had found out we were not human. At the end of his story, the heroine and the hero of the book fell in love and lived happily ever after. *Is that what he was hoping for us or am I reading too much into this?*

A letter came for me just before lunch time. It simply and cryptically read, "You have no idea who they are. Be careful and know that we are not the evil that they say we are." Ok. So, this was a new spin that was totally unexpected. *What was I supposed to think about this?* I barely knew this family that had suddenly decided that it was their duty to take on my safety, and I was learning all these things about myself that no one seemed fit to tell me until now. How was I supposed to know who to trust? But deep down, I really felt that I could trust them. I felt safe when I was with them and my instincts hadn't failed me so far in life. I decided that when Xander or Alaric picked me up after work I would trust them enough to tell them about this newest development. I hoped that I was doing the right thing.

Just like clockwork, Alaric was waiting for me at the door when I was ready to go home, I had to wonder what my nosy co-workers thought about me going home with two different guys this week, Jennifer from accounting was staring at Alaric like he was the buffet and she was starving. She was also shooting daggers at me. I wanted to feel smug, but with all the turmoil, I just felt drained. I gave her a smile that didn't reach my eyes and continued walking.

I told Alaric about the note. He seemed more captivated about the way they were trying to get me to distrust them more than he was concerned. " I wouldn't worry about it. They are just trying a different angle since they know they can't come at you directly without a fight from all of us."

His signature mustang was not in the parking lot, so I looked at him inquiringly.

"I thought it would just be best if we drove together. I have never driven a soccer mom car before." He winked as he took the keys from me. I knew that I should at least act offended, but all I could do was laugh.

"That is the reaction I was hoping to get. You should really laugh more often, your whole face lights up when you laugh." He smiled at me warmly and it was hard not to smile back. If he was trying to get me to relax, it was working. I sat back in the passenger seat and took a deep breath and let my shoulders drop from their tense state.

"You know, you make a cute soccer mom." I said to Alaric. He cracked the most genuine smile I had ever seen. It wasn't his usual sexy grin, it was an actual smile complete with teeth and everything. He looked truly content and that just made my heart melt. If he turned out to be my soul mate, it wouldn't be such a bad thing.

"Where are we headed?" I asked him as we started driving away from work.

" I figured we could go through a drive through and grab some food and head back to your place. I know that we should keep digging into your powers and why the Crissnas are so hell bent on attacking you, but after last night I figured you need a night off from the heavy conversations. We can just spend some time relaxing at your place, maybe even watch some television."

Right now that sounded as perfect as it could be. I nodded and we headed for some chicken to take home. We talked about mundane things on the way there. A couple of times, he reached his hand over and placed it over mine as he drove. It was very comforting and it was easy to be with him, but there was also that undercurrent of sexual tension that threatened to pull me under. I wondered if it was the same for him.

When we got to my house, I had this eerie feeling that we were being watched. I didn't see anyone and I didn't foresee anything happening, but the feeling was there nonetheless. Alaric tuned into what I was feeling, and did a thorough sweep of the house and the grounds and didn't find anything out of place. It was probably just the stress of everything weighing on me.

We entered the kitchen side by side and I set up the food while he got us some drinks and napkins. We sat across from each other and I watched him while I was eating. He seemed very at ease with himself and everything around him. He made small talk while we ate and smiled often. He had a great sense of humor, which was as much surprising as it was alluring. He always seemed so dangerous and electrifying, his humor made him seem more human and approachable.

When we were finished eating, he suggested that I go and make myself more comfortable while he cleaned up the kitchen. I walked into my room and changed into some joggers and a t- shirt, which was much less constricting than my work clothes. I let my hair down from my updo that I always wore to work and let it flow down my back. I knew it was not my most attractive look, but I was really just going for comfort.

Despite everything that was happening, it was gratifying to be able to let down my guard with Alaric. There was that deep attraction there, but it was more than that, he is someone that can be trusted and would care for me. I have never trusted effortlessly, that is easy to see from the amount of friends that I have to the amount of meaningful relationships I have formed. I always felt that the only person I could ever truly rely on was my mom and even though she deceived me about all of this, I understood. I know she was just trying to keep me safe and allow for us both to have a normal life. This life that I am choosing, it is not normal, nor will it ever be. I now understand that as long as I stay with other Vampires I won't continue to age. I am not sure what that will mean for me in the long term. I have always wanted to do everything I want to do now because I knew I was not guaranteed a tomorrow, especially since my mom passed away. I began to take life a little more seriously because it is definitive, there is an end. Now, to know that there may never be an end both gives me excited goosebumps and a little bit of trepidation. *If I don't fit in or find my place with other Vampires, then what will eternity be like?* Both Alaric and Xander somehow believe they are both my soul mates. That is an impossibility and what if things don't work out with Alaric, what will become of me?

All of this was just too much to consider all at once, I am a strong person but this is a lot for anyone to truly absorb this quickly. I just needed to spend some time with Alaric, figure out if there was more than just lust there between us. I also needed to learn as much as I could about my powers and why the Crissnas are so hell bent on destroying me. I am not a threat to anyone, nor do I want to be. I need to maintain as much normal in my suddenly abnormal life as possible. Maybe I should have Lindsey over to spend a girl's night. Just then, I needed to get back in there to Alaric before he sent out a search party for me.

When I returned to the living room, he had some blankets on the couch, a roaring fire in the fireplace, and he was flipping through the books on my coffee table. He looked up the second I entered the room and that beautiful lopsided grin was present on his gorgeous face. My cheeks went up in flames thinking about what I would like to do with him and his grin kicked up a notch. I needed to start remembering that he can hear my thoughts when they are too loud. He stood up and reached out to me. I didn't hesitate to sit next to him and he covered my lap with the blanket that we were then sharing. It was very soft and I wanted to reach out and touch his face to see if it compared.

"I know this is a lot for you. I have had years to know and understand what my dreams about you were about. I waited over a hundred years for you to materialize. I knew that one day I would find the one for me, it was really difficult to be patient, but here you are. When I knew you were in danger because of your circumstances and Xander and I began watching you, it was so arduous to not reach out to you. I saw in your eyes and in your actions how losing your mom affected you. I wanted to hold you and tell you that everything was going to be ok. She was a strong woman who chose to leave this earth and protect you as long as she could from our kind of life. It isn't easy to live for eternity with enemies like the Crissnas. It is sometimes very boring because you already know and have learned so much, it is a constant quest to find new adventures to keep you busy and content. I am so grateful that I have my family there for me and now you. I feel like my life is now exactly as it should be. I will do anything for you and protect you from everything. I want you in my life, as my life. I know this is a lot for you to digest but just think about it all. I have all the time in the world, I will never push you past what you are able to give me. I hope one day you will give me your heart."

I reached out and smoothed my palm over his cheek to find that it was indeed softer than I thought. My eyes lingered on his full lips wanting to press my own to them. He must have seen my hesitancy because he leaned in toward me but allowed me to take the next step. I looked into his eyes that were burning and hooded and I moved that last centimeter and kissed him. It was all consuming, it was everything. His lips parted and our tongues intertwined. I felt engulfed in something I had never felt before and I was in his lap before I even realized it. It was like I could not get close enough to him. He moved the blanket aside and leaned down so I was on top of him kissing him and I was consumed with fire. I could feel parts of my body tingling and begging me to allow his touch. I reached down and slowly, inch by inch raised his shirt up until he scooted up enough to take it off completely. He was all muscle, I ached to run my hands along his taut abs.

There were warning bells going off somewhere deep inside of me. This was too soon. He knew so much more about me than I knew about him. I had only really gotten to know him and his family in less than two weeks. I needed time to make sure this was right.Finally, those warning bells won the internal fight. I eased off of him and he stared at me with a hooded, glazed look. He grasped my arms lightly, just enough to keep me in place. "What's wrong?"

"Alaric, I want you, more than I have ever wanted anything but I feel a little bit of a disadvantage here. You have been watching me for years and knew the dreams were really premonitions. I have been dreaming about you and Xander for just as long, but for me this was never a reality until just days ago. I need to make sure for myself that this is right before I dive right in. I know this sounds ridiculous and most women would be falling over each other to have a chance at being with you, but I am the type of person that needs to make sure this is really something more than lust before I take that turn. I am sorry."

I looked down expecting him to get angry or tell me that this is 2022 and people have sex all the time and it is not as big of a deal as I making it out to be. But instead, he looked at me with the kindest expression and lifted the blanket up and patted the spot next to him. "How about we just cuddle and talk and really get to know each other. I get where you are coming from, I would never push you to give more than you are ready to give. I know we are meant to be, so I can be patient."

I snuggled up next to his warmth and he placed his arm around me so I could lay on his chest. I had to settle my hormones for a minute before I could talk. We ended up talking through most of the night about everything from family to our childhoods to our dreams. It turned out that we had a lot more in common than I ever thought we could. Of course, his childhood was spent with parents and siblings who really cared and I only had a mom who cared, but there were still a lot of similarities. We liked a lot of the same things. We both wanted to adventure and travel and get out of any comfort zones we had made for ourselves. We had the same morals and we both loved the same kind of music and art. I could not have dreamed up a better man for me if I tried.

Talking and laughing with him well into the morning before a roaring fire, I had the best time I had with a man without having sex in my life. I had no idea how much time had passed until I started yawning and realized it was four in the morning.

"Go get some sleep or if you would like, feel free to sleep here. I will still be here when you wake up. It is the weekend, I have no place I would rather be."

As tempting as it was to just stay there on the couch with him, I knew I needed to have a little separation so I gave him a kiss on the cheek and headed to my bed for a few hours of sleep before I had to start the day. I slept better than I had in a long time and I didn't have the normal dream.

At around nine, I decided it was time to start the day. I showered and got ready as quickly as I could and walked out quietly so I wouldn't wake Alaric. He was just folding the blankets on the couch. He had his back to me and I watched in fascination as the muscles in his back rippled under his skin as he folded the blankets. When he was finished, he bent over and put his shirt back on. It was difficult to not sign audibly in frustration. "Good morning Phoebe. Did you sleep well?"

"As a matter of fact, I did. How about you?"

"Slept like a baby. So, I would love to take you out for some breakfast after I use the restroom and make myself presentable." He waited for my nod and passed by brushing my side as he walked to the restroom. Everytime I looked at him or touched him, it was like lightning was in my veins. I longed to touch him more, hold on, and never let go. We went to a little diner that I enjoy. I really wasn't in the mood for something upscale. Alaric was probably used to places like that, but I definitely wasn't. A diner was more my pace, it felt more comfortable. The diner was decorated in what I would consider a fifties style. There were stainless steel bar stools upholstered red on top near the counter. The booths had tiny jukeboxes at each one and I briefly wondered if they worked or were just for decoration. The walls were covered in posters of celebrities and singers from the past from the fifties to the seventies and there were a few Elvis records on the walls. It was a place my mom would have adored. The smell of bacon and coffee wafted through the air making my stomach growl.

We ordered some eggs and fruit and talked a bit about everything and nothing at all as we sipped our coffee. We were somewhat limited on topics at a public venue. It was just enjoyable being around him. We could be talking about the weather and he could make it sexy and interesting.

"I really would like to spend some more time honing my skills and talking with your family. I want to know everything that I can about all of you and the *other team*. I would like to figure out why they are trying to get to me so desperately and even going as far as to send me notes at work. It freaked me out when they came for us at your home. Quite honestly, the night on the road and the note scared me more because both times I was alone, until you and Xander came along."

He placed his hand over mine trying to be comforting, but again it just gave a jolt to my system. "We can spend as much time with my family as you want. We can practice your skills and discuss whatever you need to in order to make you feel safer."

"Thank you." I made the mistake of looking into his eyes and the look of concern that I saw there made me want to jump across the booth and kiss him. The waitress brought us our check as she checked him out and we paid and headed to his family home.

"So the Crissnas, tell me why you think they are trying so hard to get to me." I said as soon as we got in the car.

"I really don't understand it myself. We have all talked about everything. We assumed they were trying to get to you because you didn't know what you were and they figured you would be easy to dispose of. They hate all Vampires and blame all of us for their deficiencies. They are angry that they don't have the abilities that we do. There is nothing that we can do to help them or to change that and I wish they would just try to live harmoniously. We have an issue with how they feed, but if they would only feed from animals then we wouldn't have any issues with them at all. They can survive on that but they refuse to, as if it is beneath them. The fact that they are constantly making more Crissnas by biting humans is also a major problem for us as well. We don't believe that is right. I am not sure how to really solve the issues between all of us. I am not sure why they keep trying to go after you now that they know you are aware of who you are and the fact that my family is protecting you. That should be enough to force them to loosen their grip on you and walk away. It should be obvious to them that you are not going to allow yourself to be taken in by them and you know how to defend yourself. I just don't get it. " He said all this and sighed and shook his head like it just didn't make any plausible sense to him at all.

"Tell me what you know about the Crissnas, please."

"They have been around about as long as we have. You already know how they become a Crissna, and how they feed to survive. They also cannot survive direct sunlight, so they slink around in the dark looking for their victims. They are responsible for a lot of the crime that goes on because they are so fast, they are not easily caught. They are restless with their limitations and the fact that speed, strength, and immortality seem to be their only benefits, unlike us who have gifts or abilities beyond those. There are some factions that try to live peacefully. They may choose to feed from a victim without killing them or turning them. They may even choose to feed from animals. They even get night shift jobs and try to acclimate to their environment and have human friends. Then, there is an even larger group of Crissnas who are lawless, kill, feed, and turn humans. That is the group that despises us and wants to eradicate our kind from the earth. They try to find us when we are younger and have not come into our powers or when we are vulnerable and away from others of our kind. Your mom took a real risk by staying away. If she had been found out, the Crissnas could have easily killed you both. I don't know how she was able to hide you for so long, but the moment you began getting your powers they were on your trail."

" I would love to solve that puzzle, but she never told me anything. I wish that she had, it would have saved a lot of confusion. I am sure she had her reasons though, she never did anything without having a very good reason for it." I said this with confidence even though my conviction that she had good reasons was dwindling. "So, all Vampires have abilities but they are all different, is that correct?"

"I am sure some of us have abilities in common, but most have one or two abilities such as seeing into the mind's of others, telekinesis, mind control, the list goes on. Some, like you and Alyssa, can do physical things with your mind like your blue light and her wind power."

"We also start having dreams of our soul mate, as you have experienced. This prepares us for what is to come and allows us to find one another. I think we are all still trying to figure out how and why you have more abilities. We still don't know what your potential might be, since you are still discovering new things about yourself. You're a bit of a conundrum, but in a good way."

"When you were talking about the faction of Crissnas that feeds on humans without turning them, how is that possible? I thought a bite was what would turn them if they didn't die from being fed on."

"It is a little more complicated than that. When a Crissna wants to turn a human, they can only bite them and inject venom without feeding on them. It is difficult to do. Once you bite a human, it's difficult to hold back because a kind of frenzy overcomes you. The only way to describe it is if you were without water for days and you were finally given the chance to drink a large amount of water but you are told to just put some in your mouth and spit it back out. It would take an enormous amount of willpower to do that."

Before I had time to really digest all of that, we were pulling through the gates of his family's home. I wondered what today would be like and if I would find out anything new about myself or them. Again, in a blur, Alaric was around to my side of the car opening the door before I even realized the car had turned off. He was such a gentleman, probably because of his age. I didn't know many men my age that bothered to do things like that for women anymore. Some of them would let the door fall in your face before they would hold it for you. So, Alaric was a breath of fresh air. I tried not to think about the fact that he was as old as he was, since he looked young and I wanted to tear his clothes off everytime I looked at him.

"Hello Phoebe!" Belle yelled as she draped her arms around me in a warm welcome. That was going to take some getting used to. The only other person who used to do that was my mom. Having Belle embrace me like that was comforting, but also made me miss my mom even more.

"How are you?" I asked as she let go of me.

"I am doing well. Thank you for asking. We are all so glad that you are here." With that she ushered me into the house.

Alyssa practically bounced into the room, much like Tigger from *Winnie the Pooh*. My thoughts must have transmitted to Alaric because in my mind he was singing the Tigger song and when I looked at him he was grinning from ear to ear. Alyssa looked from me to Alaric, got a secret smile on her face, and invited me into the family room. She put her arm around me as we walked in as if we had been friends forever. To be honest though, it actually felt like we had been. There was just something about her that was endearing and I knew we would end up being best friends.

The entire family was sitting there, talking and laughing. I knew it was crazy, but I had this yearning to be a part of the family. I wished nothing more than to be with them, talking and laughing at some inside joke that only we understood. I would be nestled in Alaric's arms, feeling the kind of warmth that only the love of family can provide. Alaric must have picked up on my thoughts. He looked at me longingly and told me in my mind, "I want that too."

We sat down together on the oversized chair. Alyssa sat across from us, their parents next to her, and Xander was sitting as far away as possible. It was like he smelled something rotting and didn't want to get any closer to it if he didn't have to. I know he positioned himself this way to avoid me. We hadn't talked much since everything had happened. I felt culpable, but I didn't know what to do to make that situation any better at the moment. My feelings for Alaric grew every day and my feelings for Xander stayed luke warm. It wasn't that I didn't like him, I did. It was just that I thought he was a genuinely nice person and I cared for him, but not in the way I cared for Alaric and I knew that was what he wanted.

"So, how have you been?" Steven asked. "Anything new that we need to know about?""Not really. No new powers and no more notes yet from the Crissnas. I just really wish I could get to the bottom of why they want to get to me so desperately. I also want to discover what I can do and really get a grip on my powers. I want to get to know all of you too. I feel like I come over and we practice but I never get to really get to know anyone."

Belle beamed, Steven smiled, Alyssa made a squealy sound, and Alaric hugged me close. Xander looked like he had just eaten a lemon. I was surprised at everyone's reaction to such a simple statement.

"We want to get to know you too. You are going to be family, and you are already starting to feel like family. You are always welcome here." Belle stated.

Now it was my turn to be a little startled. I hadn't really considered that this would eventually be my family. After all, Alaric is my soulmate, or Xander is?!? If I had to choose a family, they are the ones I would want. I have never seen a family that close- knit before. It was what I always wanted when I was growing up.

Xander popped up and suggested we all get started on perfecting my abilities. I was ready to get started anyway.

" I should probably mention that I am sometimes able to see things that have already happened when I am with certain people. I think maybe it is their memories or thoughts. I am not really sure. I should have mentioned it before but I wasn't sure if maybe I was just imagining it. Everyone sat back down. Maybe I should have only mentioned this to Alaric when we were alone. The cat was out of the bag now, so I would have to just deal with it.

They all looked amazed at what I was saying. "What certain people? What exactly are you seeing that you think are memories or thoughts?" Steven asked.

"Well...I see certain things about myself but it is from a different perspective. I can see myself when I was younger going to school, walking to my car, that sort of thing. I also can feel what the other person is feeling about those memories or thoughts."

"If you are seeing these things about yourself, how do you know it is not somehow coming from you?" Xander asked. He seemed very uncomfortable and began shifting in his seat.

At this point, Alaric picked up on what was happening. He was able to see the images I was thinking of flitting through my mind. "Those are my memories you are seeing. But when...?"

I immediately thought of when we would kiss and he stopped speaking and just smiled. "I think there are times when I am thinking about memories of her and she is able to pick up on that." He said to save me from being embarrassed.

"Think of a memory or something about her and see if she is able to see it." Alyssa suggested.

Alaric looked at me and said, "I don't think it exactly works that way, Alyssa. She and I can work on that skill later. How about we go outside and work on her blue fire instead?"

Everyone let it go, but I knew it was only a temporary reprieve. . I would have to explain that it only happened when Alaric and I were being intimate and that was a difficult thing to explain to his family. I was afraid of his parents' reaction but most afraid of Xander's. He didn't know that Alaric and I had become closer and I didn't want to hurt his feelings. I was glad for being spared from that conversation, however brief.

We all walked outside, it was a beautiful day and the sun was bright in the sky. Beams of light filtered through the trees, and the forest was alive with the sounds of animals scurrying about. I practiced sending my blue fire to various places throughout the forest and Alyssa would use her wind power to suck up all the oxygen and put it out. I was starting to be able to do this with ease. I didn't have to really concentrate as I had to before. I just looked at where I wanted to aim and pictured it and it happened. I was also able to control how big of a burst I was able to send. It was almost like second nature and that was a little frightening considering I only knew I had this power for such a short time.

Xander suggested that we test my speed, so he, Alaric, Alyssa, and I ran throughout the forest. It was crazy. I could feel the wind in my face and my long hair was blowing behind me. It felt like just seconds and we were almost a mile from the house. I was able to keep up with everyone and even run a little faster than Alyssa. I kept looking to my left and to my right to see where everyone else was. I could see Alaric right beside me on my left giving me the thumbs up. Running this fast was so effortless that he was able to concentrate on giving me the thumbs up, turning sideways, smiling and continuing to run without missing a beat. Xander was on my right and Alyssa was just a few steps behind him. He was looking straight ahead and seemed very focused. It seemed to me like everything was happening in slow motion. I noticed everything as I ran. I could hear the animals scuttling around on the forest floor, the birds chirping in the trees, and I could smell the wet dew and the moss on the trees. When we reached our stopping point, none of us were out of breath.

Alyssa hopped over to me and hugged me. "You are amazing! It took us a long time to reach this speed. Have you tried running this fast before?""No, I never thought I could." I replied feeling a little proud of myself.

"Bet you can't beat me back there." Alaric said as he winked and headed back like he was *The Flash*.

"Oh no you don't!" I yelled as I ran just a bit past him feeling victorious and a little giddy. I felt so free running like this and having this time with him and his family. Suddenly, I had a blinding flash of a man standing before me. He was regal, dressed in an expensive suit. He had a brushing of gray hair at his temples and sparkling blue eyes. He smiled at me and told me that he was so excited to have his daughter back in his life but his mouth never moved. I stopped running and the vision cleared. It took everyone a few seconds to realize I had stopped and they all trotted back to me.

Alaric put his arm around me. "Have you ever seen that man before?"

"What man?" Alyssa asked.

I took a deep breath to clear my thoughts. I explained to them the vision that I had just experienced. I had no idea who he was, but he somehow looked familiar. I just couldn't place him. I shook my head in frustration. "What was that? Was that someone communicating with me, a premonition, or am I just going a little nuts?"

"We should get you back to our parents. They will be able to make sense of this." Xander suggested. He turned away and headed to the house. Alyssa patted my arm sympathetically and went back to the house while Alaric put his arm around me and we took our time getting back. I think he could sense that I was more than a bit shaken by what had just happened.

When we entered the living room and his parents saw us, they immediately asked everyone to sit down and tell them what was wrong. I explained what had happened when I was running back to the house.

Steven's face crinkled in worry. "Phoebe, I am not really sure what that was. It could be that your father is alive and his gift is being able to communicate through your mind. It could also be a premonition of something that is yet to come to pass. I will do a little research and see what I may be able to find out. If you have any other visions, please let me know." He got up, patted my arm, and walked toward his study.

"Is anyone hungry?" Belle asked.

We all collectively declined any food.

" I should probably be getting back to my house. I have a lot to think about." I said. I really wanted to spend more time with them, as I had intended, but the vision, or whatever it was, had me feeling like I wanted to be alone to digest all of it.

Alaric immediately got up and offered to take me home. I hugged Alyssa and Belle to say goodbye. When I was finished, Xander had vanished. Alaric and I headed to the car and before he opened my door, he stopped in front of me and enveloped me in his strong arms. He seemed to know just what I needed. We stood there like that for what seemed forever. I was content to just lay my head on his chest and listen to his heart beat as his warmth seeped into me, calming my rapidly beating heart. He took a step back and kissed my forehead and ushered me into the car.

Chapter 7- Lindsey

We talked about little insignificant things on the way to my house. It was nice to have a normal conversation, and not have to discuss my abilities or my growing attraction to Alaric. When we arrived, Lindsey's car was in my driveway. Oh crap! I had been ignoring her texts because so many things had been happening. She was probably here to make sure I am not dead in a ditch somewhere.

She quickly got out of her car as soon as we drove up. When Alaric got out and opened the door for me, she looked like she wanted to spit fire. "Where have you been? I have been texting and calling you." She said this while standing with her hand on her hip and her foot was tapping the gravel so quickly, I was surprised it wasn't getting pounded into dirt.

"I am so sorry. My phone has been dead and I have been spending some time with Alaric. You remember Alaric?" I indicated the completely hot man standing so close to me I could feel his body heat.

He extended his hand to Lindsey and she ignored it. Instead, she ungraciously grabbed a hold of my arm and dragged me toward my house as she yelled goodbye to him.

"Alaric is not going anywhere Lindsey. He is over to spend some time with me. You are welcome to come in and join us. I can make us some lunch." She didn't look too keen on that idea but she accepted begrudgingly. Alaric took the hint and followed us into the house.

"On second thought, how about I order us some lunch? The Pizza Pan delivers out this far. What would you both like on your pizza?"

"Anything for me is fine. Thank you Phoebe." Alaric said as he brushed an errant hair from my face. His touch made my nerve endings feel raw.

"I would like a veggie pizza." said Lindsey as she pouted near the door.

I ordered the pizza and we all sat down on the couch to wait.

"So, I thought that you didn't know who Alaric was. How did you two end up finding each other?""Crazy story really..I am editing his first novel. We met when he came in for some pointers, which he didn't need. He is very talented, his book will be a hit." I gazed over at Alaric and he was giving me that lopsided grin I had grown to love. Lindsey was looking between the two of us like we had just sprouted three heads.

"Phoebe, do you think you can help me freshen up in your bathroom? I am sure Alaric won't mind waiting, will you Alaric?" She stated, a little snappy, while she stood up and waited for me to answer her command. I looked at Alaric and apologized to him in my mind for her rude behavior. I let him know that I wasn't sure what had come over her. She usually wasn't like this.

He told me not to worry and Lindsey and I walked to the bathroom. As soon as we got in there she started grilling me. "What the hell? You make out with him a few weeks ago and then see him again, and start acting all love struck? I have never seen you act that way with a guy before. Are you sleeping with him?"

"Wow! I love you Lindsey but really what has gotten into you? I really like Alaric and it is truly none of your business if I have slept with him or not.""Well, I guess that answers that question." she said as she tapped her fingernails against the counter.

"Look, you are my best friend and he is my, well I am not sure what yet but he means a lot to me. I would like for the two of you to be able to get along. He has been nice to you, there is no reason for you to be so rude."

Lindsey changed her entire demeanor. "Of course you're right. I don't know what got into me. I guess when I couldn't get a hold of you for several days I just got worried and I took it out on him. I will be nice."

We walked back into the living room and shortly after, our pizza arrived. We ate and talked. I still felt like Lindsey was grilling him about everything from his parents to what he does for a living besides writing novels. I felt it was very intrusive and I was beginning to get pretty irritated. She then suggested that we all go out to the club for a while. I think we both agreed just to get her to stop asking questions.

Lindsey drove her car and Alaric drove us to the club in mine.

"I am so sorry again. She promised she was going to be nice and then she started asking you twenty questions. I have never seen her act this way before."

"Nothing to worry about Phoebe. I am sure she is just worried about you." he said but his words and his expression didn't match. He seemed like he was either upset or concerned about all of her questions and nasty attitude.

"We don't have to stay long."

"It is ok. I know how you love to dance and honestly I love to watch you dance. You seem so relaxed and free. That is the way I want you to be able to feel all the time. I am hoping to make that a reality for you soon."

Ok, so when a gorgeous man, who incidentally is supposed to be your soul mate, basically offers you the world, it is difficult not to melt into a gooey puddle. It took everything in me not to make him pull over to the side of the road and make him mine in every way. I am sure he could feel what I was feeling because he gave me a wicked smile and kissed the back of my hand in a sensuous way.

We arrived at the club and Alaric escorted both of us inside like a gentleman. Lindsey immediately asked him to get us drinks and dragged me to the dance floor. Alaric just raised his eyebrows but he proceeded to the bar.

"I don't think this guy is right for you. There is something just off about him. Why don't we just wait for a bit and then just sneak out without him?"

"Absolutely not! I appreciate that you are concerned, really I do, but he is very important to me. . I am getting to know not just him but also his entire family and I adore them all."This just seemed to make her more pissed off. She stalked away and went up to the second floor to dance. I started to look for Alaric, but he was already headed my way with our drinks. We looked for a table and he offered to bring Lindsey's drink to her but I told him to just let it go. We sat there for a while watching everyone gyrate to the beat of the music. It was intoxicating. After we finished our drinks, one of my favorite songs came on, so he invited me to the dance floor.

It was like deja vu being in his arms on the dance floor again. He wrapped one arm around my waist and the other held my hand and he pulled me close. I rested my head against the hard muscles of his chest and we moved slowly to the song. I decided right then and there that I didn't know what I was waiting for. This was definitely not just lust, I was starting to fall in love with this man. I don't know when it happened, but it had. He was everything I had ever dreamed of, literally and figuratively. He was kind, loved his family, we had a lot in common, and I was pretty sure he was falling for me as well.

I looked up into his eyes and I am sure he knew everything I was thinking."I know this is early, but I too know what I feel. I am in love with you Phoebe."

"I love you too Alaric."

He pulled me in for the sweetest kiss. I felt like I was drunk, the world didn't matter, just him. Everything around us just melted into the background. When he pulled away slightly, I could see the love and longing in his eyes.

" I am going to go tell Lindsey that I am tired and you are going to drive me home." He responded by kissing me on the forehead and I went to find Lindsey. She was not hard to find, she had no less than three guys dancing around her. I pushed my way through the crowd and told her I was leaving. For a moment, I thought she was going to protest but she just waved me off and told me we would talk later. I still didn't understand her attitude but now was not the time to figure it out. Now, all my time was for Alaric and I couldn't wait to get him home.

Alaric joined me as I was leaving the dance floor. He tucked my arm into his elbow and we made our way to the car. I knew that we were both more than ready to get to my house. We didn't talk much on the drive, both of us lost in our own thoughts. He did, however, hold my hand all the way home.

Chapter 8- The Next Step

We both knew what was going to happen when we got into my house and the anticipation was killing me. We finally arrived, and he was even faster getting to my door to let me out. Once the car door was closed, he held my hand and pulled me close. We both stared at each other, there was an intensity in his eyes that I hadn't seen before. I studied his full lips and reached out with my fingers to trace them. That was all that it took. He bridged the gap between us and his lips seared into mine. The kiss was setting me on fire. He turned me around so I was flush against the car door and he pressed my head back and rained fiery kisses along my neck to the sensitive spot just below my ear. I wrapped my legs around him and he quickly carried me into the house and onto my bed.

He pulled my shirt up over my head and his lips were between my breasts. I ached everywhere and my body arched toward him to give him greater access. He seared a trail down and unzipped my pants slowly with his teeth and then inch by inch pulled them off of me. He raised back up and I pulled his shirt from him. His body was so beautiful, he was all muscles and abs. I reached out and splayed my fingers over his abdomen and pulled him in for another scorching kiss. He pulled his pants off and rained kisses lower and lower until he was pulling my panties off and they lay useless on the floor. He kissed me between my thighs and I was soon crying out in ecstasy.

"I want you, please." I pleaded. He was hovering over me and entered me with a passionate rhythm that was all Alaric. He kissed me as he drove into me over and over. My body arched as I screamed out his name and found my release as he found his. Once we were spent, he looked down at me, moving the hair from my cheeks. He kissed me sweetly and said, "That was worth all those years of waiting for you. I never knew it could be so wonderful. I love you so much." His blue eyes pierced into me as I told him I love him too. He moved to the side and pulled me close to him to lay on his chest.

It had never been this way with anyone before. I lay there totally fulfilled, wondering if it would always be this amazing. This man loves me as much as I love him. Only he waited for me for a century to be his. This was what all my dreams had been leading me to. This perfect man that in the span of less than two weeks, I had grown to love more than anything. I wistfully wondered how I had ever gotten so lucky. I could feel his breathing getting steady and even. I peered at his closed eyes and peaceful face and thought to myself that I knew he was my soulmate. He was just right for me. I drifted off to sleep with a smile on my lips.

Chapter Seven

A New Life

I woke up in the morning feeling better than I ever had. I slept well and I was intertwined with Alaric. My head was on his chest and his arm was around my shoulders and his leg was slung across mine. He woke up when I raised my head to look at him. I was suddenly shy and afraid I looked terrible in the morning. I tried to comb my fingers through my hair as I was sure it looked like a bird had made its nest there overnight. He just chuckled and pulled me to him for a kiss telling me I looked beautiful. I am sure I didn't believe him but it put me at ease anyway.

"How are you feeling this morning, my love?" he asked.

"I feel wonderful. That is the best I have slept in years and of course last night was beyond amazing."

"That is just what every man loves to hear." he grinned that obscene lopsided grin that just made me want to repeat last night all over again. "We should really get back to my house and see what my parents have been able to figure out."

I reluctantly got up, and headed in for a quick shower. I kept remembering every moment of last night and the way his skin felt against mine. I didn't know why I had waited but he was worth the wait. To say that he was skilled was an understatement. He made me feel things that I didn't even know were possible. I really do love this man! I felt like a school girl when her first crush admitted he liked her too. There were butterflies in my stomach just thinking about him being in the next room, in my bed. It wasn't just lust or a physical attraction, he really understood me. I know we were still getting to know each other, but even couples that have been together for years are always still discovering things about one another.

After my shower, I put on some light makeup and dried my hair. I kept expecting him to knock on the door or just come in but he didn't. He was giving me my space to get ready. When I was finished, I walked back into the bedroom just in time to see him stand up in all his glory to put his clothes on. Damn! I was never going to get used to this. He was magnificent, they should use his image to carve statues.

I know he felt what I was feeling because he gave me that grin of his. He put on his pants and they rode so low on his body I could see that sexy v shape below his extraordinary abs. I wanted to run my hands all over them and throw him back in the bed. I reminded myself that we had things to do.

"Don't worry. I want you too. We have all eternity to explore each other, get to know one another, and just be. I love you. "

I didn't know that it was possible to feel such euphoria. Those three simple words put together and spoken from the lips of Alaric were weaving a magical spell around my heart. "I love you too!"

He held me tight, as if I was the only thing saving him from not drowning in an ocean of emotion. I felt safe in his arms and finally felt like I had found my place. I fit in with his family, and I loved and adored him. It all happened so fast, but I didn't have doubts. We stayed like that for a few minutes, lost in each other's arms and our own thoughts, then it was time to face the day.

Before we had a chance, my cell phone rang. It was Lindsey. I hesitated even answering, given her recent attitude but I figured if I didn't answer she might come over here again like last time. "Hey, Lindsey. What's up?"

"Look Phoebe, I know you are probably a little pissed off at me right now but I have a reason for my behavior. I really need to talk to you, alone and soon. It is really important and probably something we should have talked about a long time ago."

"I am getting ready to go to Alaric's house in a bit. Can it wait until later?"

"NO! I need to talk to you now and it can't be over the phone. Can I just come over?"

I looked at Alaric and he seemed to have heard everything. He gave me a nod and started to get up and get dressed.

"Sure Lindsey. Come on over."

She hung up before she even said goodbye. She was getting stranger by the day. I have known her since we were young, I couldn't fathom what was going on with her.

"I'm so sorry Alaric. I still want to come over and spend the day with you and your family. Is it ok if we put it off for an hour or so?"

"Of course." he said as he kissed me on top of the head. "Is it ok with you if I borrow the car? I have a few errands I can run in town and you can text me when you are ready to go to my house." "That sounds perfect. I will make sure to get this conversation with Lindsey over with as quickly as possible." I kissed him until I could feel the warmth spreading throughout my entire body, then sadly broke off the kiss so he could complete his errands and get back here quickly.

Before I knew it, she was over. I was still drying my hair, but by the look on her face that would have to wait. She came in like a hail storm and sat on the couch with a cloud of doom and gloom hanging over her head. I really hoped that this was not going to be another Alaric lecture. I loved Lindsey, but really enough was enough.

She pursed her pink lips and gestured for me to sit down beside her. Her hands were shaking like leaves in a fall breeze and she started pinching her lips together in a fine line so much that they almost disappeared.

"Whatever it is, just tell me. The anticipation is killing me and apparently you as well."

"Ok, look, this is going to be a big shock and I need you to hear me out before you say anything." She looked at me beseechingly for confirmation that I would hear her out. I made the gesture of zipping my lips shut and throwing away the key. That normally would have made her laugh, but she only grimaced. Her eyes darted around the room. "We are alone, right?"

"Yes, Alaric had to run some errands in town." I waited impatiently for her to begin. I started tapping my fingers against my thigh and looking at her with my eyebrows raised in silent questioning.

"I know that you have recently learned that you are a Vampire." If she would have said that she secretly had multiple personality disorder, it couldn't have surprised me more. I instinctively jumped off the couch ready to deny everything when she calmly gestured for me to sit.

"Look, I am still the same Lindsey that you have known for years. You can trust me. Sit down and I will explain everything."

I sat down but I could feel the adrenaline pumping through my veins. My senses were raised. I could hear the water in the kitchen sink drip slowly and quietly. I could almost smell the fear coming from Lindsey as she tried to formulate a sentence to tell me what was going on.

"I have known what you were since we met. I want you to know that I love you and you have always been my friend truly, but I was sent to keep an eye on you. We didn't meet by accident, but our friendship is real." As she said this she grabbed my cold and clammy hands in hers. I was in shock. I wouldn't have known what to say, even if I hadn't promised her to remain quiet and hear her out.

"I also know that Alaric and his family are Vampires and that your mom was also a Vampire. Your mom didn't know about me. She thought I was a normal human, or she never would have approved of our friendship. Just like Alaric and his family have been watching you, so have we. We weren't sure when you would begin to come into your powers so we waited. We didn't want to scare you, but we needed to keep you safe." This was starting to feel a little too familiar.

She waited for a response from me. "So, are you telling me you are a Vampire too?"

She looked like she was deliberating her response. "No, I am not a Vampire. I am different and I am not even sure that Alaric's family knows about my kind. I am not a Vampire and I am not a Crissna, but I am both."

"How is that even possible? Alaric has explained to me that Crissnas are made while we are born so how can you be both?"

"I was born a Vampire but while I was still in my mother's womb she was bitten and killed by a Crissna. My father found my mother near death on our kitchen floor and rushed her to the hospital. At that time, he didn't know any healing Vampires and he desperately wanted to save us both. My mother didn't make it but they were able to save me. My dad raised me as a Vampire but I started to have cravings that Vampires don't and I didn't develop any of the abilities that Vampires do. He couldn't understand it, but he thought it may have something to do with my mother dying and being attacked while I was still unborn. It wasn't until I was fourteen that I was approached by a Crissna and they were able to fill in the gaps and explain that I was a hybrid because of the way my mother was attacked. When I was fifteen, they positioned my father to change jobs so that he would end up here and it made it easier for me to befriend you when you ended up here. They wanted me to keep an eye on you to make sure you were protected from the Vampires. They are not what you think they are. They want you as a part of their race so you can be with one of their sons and keep the Vampire race going. Their numbers have been dwindling for years and they don't want their numbers to become extinct and the Crissnas to rule. Your father is a Crissna, not a Vampire. You are another hybrid, just created in a different way. Your father and mother created you out of love and you were born. Your mom and dad had a huge argument when she was still pregnant with you and she disappeared. He didn't find you until you were almost sixteen and he didn't want to frighten you by approaching you until you were ready and knew what you were."

"What the hell! Lindsey, I have no idea what to think right now." I rubbed the tense muscles in the back of my neck and stood up and paced back and forth in front of the fireplace. So many things were running through my head. I just found out that I am a Vampire, now Lindsey says that I am a hybrid. Alaric and his family never said anything about the possibility of hybrids and according to Lindsey they didn't know they existed. Lindsey is a hybrid with no Vampire powers and I am supposedly a hybrid with many Vampire powers. This was too much to handle. I was ready to have a nervous breakdown. I sat down heavily on the floor cross legged facing Lindsey with my head hung over my lap and my hands over my head. I just wanted to block it all out. I was just getting used to the idea of being a Vampire and having powers and now this bomb was dropped on me. I wanted to trust Lindsey, but to know that she was sent here to befriend me in order to keep watch over me felt like a betrayal. I really didn't know her at all. Then there was Alaric and his family. I trusted them, even though I hadn't known them for long. They felt like family. Right now, Lindsey felt like an intruder into my new world. I didn't like it and I didn't want it.

"Lindsey, you have to leave."

"What? You can't be serious? I have been your friend since we were teenagers. We have experienced everything together, and you are asking me to leave? What about Alaric? Are you going to invite him back in?" She stood up suddenly and reminded me of when we were younger and she didn't get her way. She stood there like an irate toddler that had just been told that she is not allowed to have any cookies.

"Yes, Lindsey. Right now, I am not sure how I am feeling about you. I'm sorry if that hurts you but you just turned my world upside down and it was just turned inside out weeks ago. I want you to leave. I need some time to think."

She seemed to know it was time to back down. She tried to reach out to hug me, but I shied away. I didn't want her to touch me right now. She dropped her arms and hung her head low and trudged slowly toward the door. "Don't take too long to think about all of this. Your dad is waiting to meet you and so are the rest of the Crissnas. You need to trust me." With those final words, she opened the door and disappeared.

I sat back down heavily on the couch and put the throw pillow over my face and screamed into it. It felt like the weight of the world was on my shoulders yet again. Moments later, I could feel Alaric gently lifting the pillow and gathering me into his arms. I couldn't speak but I trusted him enough to tell him what had just happened. I tried to go back through the scenario with Lindsey in my mind and project it to Alaric. He didn't say anything, but just continued to hold me close.

When I was finally calm enough, I settled back and looked into his eyes. The only emotion I saw there was concern for me and love. I didn't see deceit or guilt, and I knew that I wouldn't but it was a nice reassurance.

"What do you think about everything that Lindsey has said?"

"I have lived a long time and I have never heard of hybrids. I don't really think they exist. I don't know if your friend has been deceived or if she is trying to deceive you.

I feel it is best that we go to my family's home and discuss all of that with them, if you are ok with that."

"Yes, I trust you and your family. I cannot believe that I have been friends with Lindsey for so many years and she had been betraying me. Our entire friendship was a farce from the beginning. It has always been so hard for me to trust because of my father, the man that raised me, and I don't let people in easily. The only exceptions to that has been Lindsey and you and your family. I felt completely comfortable with her from the beginning. She was the total opposite of me, but she just always listened when I needed her to and she was always there trying to get me out of my comfort zone to enjoy life more. I never for a moment suspected that anything was out of place. I feel really stupid."

"You loved and trusted her. You are a good person, there is no reason for you to feel stupid about anything. I am sure that somewhere along the way she cared about you too. Who wouldn't?"

We soon left to go discuss this new information with his family. I had no idea what to think but I was hoping they would have some answers for me or at least know where to get some.

Chapter 9- The Plan

I was stressed all the way to their house. My fingers were worrying at the fringe of my shirt. Alaric tried to keep me calm and comforted by holding my hand. It helped a bit, but I wasn't going to stop being worried until I had answers. I really felt the bite of betrayal from Lindsey like acid in the back of my throat. I tried to think back on all the good and bad times we had together.

She was with me through my first crushes and boyfriends. She was with me when my mom died and she had stuck by my side, giving me comfort, lots of girl's nights out and girl's nights in. She even booked massages and facials for us both so I could have an entire day to just relax. She had seemed to be the most loyal friend, I didn't see any cracks in her veneer. *How could I have been so fooled by her? If she was able to fool me so easily, was my judge of character really that good?*

I had poured out my heart to her about all my feelings about mom leaving too young, and when I felt like I needed her most. I never would have made it through those dark days without her. I didn't have anyone else that I trusted enough to talk to or to be silent with when I needed to be. Her betrayal made mom's death feel like an open wound, ready to pull me down into the earth and cover me with soil never to rise again.

We pulled up in front of Alaric's family home. I was anxious to get out and ask for answers but also so afraid of what those answers might be. Alaric came around and opened my door, he helped me up by holding my small hand in his large capable one. As soon as I stood up, he placed his other hand against my cheek. I could feel the roughness of it against my sensitive skin. He tipped my chin up and kissed me softly. His full soft lips against mine made me forget everything I was worried about. My lips parted under his tender assault and he deepened the kiss. Every nerve ending felt like it was being electrified and the world dropped away. We weren't in Alaric's driveway anymore, we were in our own magical world where only we existed and all the worries floated away on the soft breeze. Too soon, our kiss ended and reality sunk in. It was time to ask for some answers.

We walked hand in hand through the beautifully manicured gardens to the front entryway. It still felt like I was walking into a mansion from the Old South, with the grand pillars on the porch. I nearly expected a matronly woman to come out with some cold glasses of lemonade. His house was like a walk through time and space.

The first person we ran into was Alyssa. She bounced over to us and kissed me on the cheek and gave Alaric a quick hug. Then she stood back and must have seen the worry in our eyes. "What's wrong? You both look like someone died."

"We have a bit of a situation to figure out. Where are mom and dad?"

"I think they were in the study. Let me go get them for you. Why don't you get Phoebe something to drink and we will all meet you in the family room?" With that she bounded out of the room, it seemed as if only the tips of her toes ever touched the ground; she was so graceful on her feet.

Alaric steered me to the family room and left momentarily to get me a drink. He came back quickly with a glass of lemonade leaving me to wonder if he saw the musings I had about his home when we first arrived. He just grinned, sat down and placed his arm around me in both a comforting and possessive way. It made me feel safe and loved, and right now, I really needed to feel that way.

Soon enough, everyone entered, first his parents, then Alyssa, and lastly Xander. He still looked like I had run over his favorite dog. I was worried about that but right now I had more concerning issues to deal with.

"We have not been able to find a lot of information about any Vampires with multiple powers. There have been some over the years, few and far between, but they were always from a royal lineage. The royal lines have been gone for years. There were so many violent fights from the Crissnas, that I have never met any royalty in my lifetime. I don't believe anyone survived the wars." Steven said. When I looked at him inquisitively he continued.

"The only people that have had multiple powers were kings and queens. They were direct descendants of the original Vampires. Some called them Royalty and others called them the Originals. Either way, they seemed to possess powers on multiple levels that none of us have ever seen before or since. About three centuries ago, there was a bloody war with the Crissnas. They had grown tired of the Vampires having powers and they especially despised the royal families because they possessed more powers than anyone else could even hope to have. They banded together and fought them. No one saw it coming and before we knew it, the royals were all dead. I have told you that one way to die is to be away from our own kind for too long, the only other way is to behead us. It takes a lot of strength and skill, we are not hard to kill and the Originals were even harder to kill. They were able to do it with sheer numbers. They lost a lot of Crissnas in that short war, but we also lost our founding families, the Originals."

"There is no way that any of them survived according to history and even some of my connections that were alive back then. If they had survived, they would have been snuffed out. The Crissnas would have made sure of that. So, we are at a loss as to how you have so many powers and we have no way of knowing if you will get more. It would be pertinent for us to find your true father. He may have some answers for you that we don't."

At this point, this was just one more mystery to be solved. I explained to them about my encounter with Lindsey that morning. This time Belle took the lead on the discussion.

"I had heard of hybrids once many years ago. I assumed it was a legend, a fantasy from some overly dramatic Vampires or Crissnas. No one that I know of has ever met a hybrid and as far as we know they don't really exist. As far as Lindsey knowing who your father is, I suppose it is possible, but he has to be a Vampire."

She must have seen the hurt in my eyes, so she added that perhaps Lindsey has been misled by someone she trusts.

"We will look into this more. I will start calling some of my contacts and we will start watching out for Lindsey, see where she goes, who she visits. Maybe that will give us some clues about all of this." Steven said.

"I know that you are feeling overwhelmed and are probably having a hard time trusting right now. You lost your mom, the only person you truly trusted, then Lindsey tells you things that couldn't be true. We come into your life and turn it upside down, and you are expected to just go with the flow. I am here to let you know, it is ok to be confused and to feel whatever you are feeling. You have been through a lot in such a short time and no one expects you to be ok with everything. If you ever need to talk, cry, scream, or question anything at all I believe I speak for all of us when I say that we are here for you whenever and no matter what the circumstances. We are your family now and we will always be here for you." Steven said. Everyone nodded their assent and one by one they came up to hug me. I really felt like they loved me. It had been a long time since I had a family and I had never had a family like this. A few tears escaped my eyes and rolled unchecked down my cheeks and Alaric held me in his arms.

"Thank you, all of you for everything you have been doing. I have never had anyone, besides my mom, who would drop everything to help me. I am so overwhelmed and humbled by your kindness. I don't know how to ever repay you for being here for me like this."

"This is what families do for each other. There is never any need to repay us for anything. You would do the same for us if the roles were reversed." Belle stated.

Alaric knew when it was time to take me home. He knew I needed to breathe. He let his family know that we were going to go back to my place to take care of some things and everyone seemed to understand, apart from Xander. He stood there and looked like he was about to cry himself and he quietly left the room. He would adjust, he would have to. We said our goodbyes and headed to the store to pick up some food items then back to my house.

"I really don't know how to handle the whole Lindsey situation. I have known her a long time and if I begin to ignore her calls, especially about something that she feels is this paramount, she is going to show up at my doorstep. I am not sure I am ready to handle her right now." I took a deep breath and I knew Alaric was about to tell me that he would handle it, but it was my problem and not his. I could not go through my life expecting someone else to handle my issues as they arose. "I just need to call her and let her know that I need some time to think."

Alaric gave me an encouraging look and a quick hug and I made the call.

"Phoebe, it is imperative that I see you right away. I know you believe you need time to think but your father really needs to see you. There is just so much you need to know and he is the only one who can tell you. We need you to trust us."

I took a deep cleansing breath. "I am hanging up now. I told you what I need and you are not listening to me."

I hung up and excused myself so I could go into the bathroom and collect myself. I stood looking at myself in the mirror. I looked tired and confused. I splashed some water on my face and decided to put Lindsey and her craziness behind me for a while.

I walked out and Alaric immediately enveloped me into his arms. He murmured soothing words into my hair as I held him tight. I breathed deeply and he smelled like sunshine and I felt at home and safe. We decided to lay on the couch and relax when there was a knock at the door. I immediately got anxious thinking that Lindsey had disregarded my feelings and showed up anyway. I wondered if she brought my so-called father with her. I was not ready to face her at this juncture but again, I was going to deal with my problems. Alaric started for the door at the same time I did and he insisted that I stand a pace behind him while he opened the door to make sure it was safe.

I stepped back and he opened the door a crack then wide open. I was surprised since I assumed it was Lindsey. Xander stepped through the door and I couldn't have been more surprised if an endangered animal had walked through and begun speaking. I stood there with my eyes wide and then recovered myself and plastered a smile on my face and welcomed him inside. I was a little shaken that he was here considering the way he has been acting since professing his undying love for me.

"Hi Xander, come on in. Can I get you anything?"

"No thank you. My parents sent me here. They got word that something was up and they wanted extra security here just in case anything untoward were to happen."

"What are they worried about?" Alaric asked.

"I am not really sure. They got a call from our cousins and Cathy had a premonition that someone was looking for us and their intentions weren't the best. She said it was still a bit fuzzy but she would keep us up to date on anything else that she sees."

"Do you think this has to do with Lindsey and everything that she is trying to sell me?" I asked both of them.

"She is not really sure but mom and dad wanted me to come over here and keep an eye on you. We are not sure if it involves you at all but the extra security is a good idea."

Well, this had the potential to get pretty awkward. Alaric and I were definitely going to have to keep our hands to ourselves as long as he was over. I only had a small couch in my living room since I hardly ever had visitors and aside from the kitchen, that was the only other place to hang out besides the bedroom and that was out of the question.

"Why don't you and Alaric have a seat in the living room and I will make us all some coffee?"

Alaric raised his eyebrow at me and thought that this was going to be awkward as he strolled into the other room. I was sure he could hear my thoughts that were the same as his. All of the sudden, my cozy home felt like a cage. There was not enough room to breathe and I could feel my anxiety well up inside me, ready to spill out at the least provocation. I could hear their easy banter from the kitchen, so at least Alaric was handling this well. I made us all some coffee and placed it on a tray, plastered on my best smile , and walked into the lion's den.

They both looked up at me expectantly as I placed the warm mugs of energy on the table. Alaric looked like he wanted to ravage me despite Xander being here. Xander looked at me longingly with his deep chocolate eyes that reminded me of a sad puppy. I realized that they had sat on opposite ends of the couch leaving the middle for me. Ugh!

I sat down and turned on the television thinking that if we just all watched a show that the awkwardness would melt away. It also gave us less time for awkward small talk. I found a comedy and we all relaxed back with our coffee. We sat like that for the duration of the movie, no one speaking to each other, but all of us laughing at the appropriate moments in the movie. I looked to my right and to my left as the movie was about to end and they both looked like there were boards attached to their backs. They sat straight up and their faces had the same looks of tension etched onto them.

As soon as the movie ended, I got up to make us a meal. Alaric got up and offered to help and Xander sat there looking like he wanted to but knew that he shouldn't intrude at the same time. He excused himself to go to the restroom while Alaric and I went into the kitchen. I breathed a sigh of relief to be out of the living room with the both of them. Alaric wrapped his arms around me from behind and squeezed the tension right out of my body. He brushed the hair off of my shoulder and replaced it with his mouth making a hot trail from my shoulder all the way to my ear. When he got there he whispered that he loved me and turned me around.

"I know this is awkward for you, having Xander here. It is not a cakewalk for me either. He is my brother and he thinks he is in love with you. I feel terrible for him. I love him. But you are mine, heart and soul and I can't give you up because he is upset. I need you." With that he swept me into his arms and kissed me with abandon. I was trying not to make too much noise even though I felt like my body was encased in fire and Alaric was the only one who could put it out. The kiss ended too quickly and left me breathless. I wanted more and as long as Xander was here, more was off limits. It was one thing to be in love with Alaric and quite another to rub Xander's face in it.

We both sighed and began making a simple meal of chicken and zucchini. Everytime our eyes met, my cheeks flooded with color as I could hear his thoughts about what he would rather be doing in the bedroom. It was difficult to concentrate on anything with him in the room.

We finally called Xander into the room to enjoy the meal in the kitchen. Dinner wasn't as uncomfortable as sitting in the living room had been. We got into the flow of a conversation about all the careers they had both had over the years. They had done so much that I had never even dreamed about and seen so many places I had only seen on a map. I still couldn't believe that I would have forever with Alaric to discover everything together. One thing that was tremendously clear was that they both loved their family without restraint. They had that in common.

As the conversation continued, I noticed that Xander always chose safer jobs that required a nurturing side while in contrast Alaric chose jobs that demanded more charisma and where he was always challenged. Alaric liked adventure and Xander seemed happy to be close to home with his family. They were alike but in some important ways polar opposites. It occurred to me that Xander was more of a homebody like me but Alaric challenged me to get out of that comfort zone and I craved that.

Once we cleared away the dishes and cleaned up the mess, I decided that I wanted to get to bed early. I planned to read for a while and I didn't want to go back into the living room and have everything go back to being awkward.

"I am not sure what to do about the sleeping arrangements, guys. The couch is really the only place besides my room. Do you two want to share my bed and I can sleep in the living room? Otherwise, someone is going to end up on the floor and I don't feel right about that at all."

Xander was the first to speak up. "I am sure that I speak for both of us when I say that it is not fair to take your bed away from you. It is not your fault that we both have to be here. I am perfectly happy to take the floor if you have some blankets perhaps." He smiled in his adorable way and looked completely sincere.

I looked at Alaric for confirmation and he nodded. I felt terrible asking either of them to sleep on the floor. "I think I may have a sleeping bag at the back of my closet. Give me a minute."

I went to my bedroom and rummaged through the closet. The rest of my house was in perfect order and very organized, but this closet was a completely different story. It looked like World War Three had broken out in there and many items of clothing and shoes were casualties laying on the soft carpeted floor. It was a miracle that I was able to find the sleeping bag. Thankfully, it still smelled like fabric softener so I brought it into the living room and set them both up with blankets and pillows. I hugged them both goodnight and headed to my bedroom. I hoped that this would not be a long term thing because for one I didn't want to deal with this level of being uncomfortable for that long and two I wasn't sure how long I could keep my hands off of Alaric. It had become natural for us to hold hands and kiss and just be natural with each other and we were both having to keep away. Then there was the fact that I couldn't invite him into my bedroom which is where we both wished he was. I needed to read and take my mind off of this situation for a while.

Chapter Eight

Things are Getting Crazy

A little after midnight, I got a text from Lindsey. I was going to completely ignore it but my curiosity got the best of me.

"You have made this very difficult for everyone. We have had to take drastic measures and for that I am sorry. We have your dad, the one you grew up with. I know that there is no love lost between the two of you but I also know that you wouldn't want anything to happen to him. If you want him released safe and sound, you will have to ditch your boyfriends and get over here. Meet me in one hour at that old abandoned cabin we used to hang out in when we were teens."

Rage like I have never felt before began flowing through my veins like molten lava. My body was heating up with it and it was causing blue sparks to fire from my hands. I needed to get it under control before I accidentally burned my little cottage down. How dare she do this! I never really knew her at all!

If I tried to go through the living room., I would end up waking the boys. I was going to have to sneak out my window like a delinquent teen running off to a party in the middle of the night. I would never forgive myself if something happened to Bob just because of me. I still loved him in a weird way because he raised me and my mom loved him so that counted for something. Damn it! I really wanted to go in there and wake them up and get their help but I didn't want Lindsey and her entourage to hurt Bob. I had to trust that Lindsey wouldn't do anything to Bob before I got there.

I had to put my walls up so my link with Alaric didn't wake him. I quietly changed into some warm clothes and slipped out the window. I didn't want to risk starting the car, so I used my newfound speed to run to the cabins she was talking about. I remembered many nights hanging out there, drinking with Lindsey and talking about everything. There was very little that I kept from her, she was my best friend. Now the place I always thought of fondly was going to represent something ugly. I hated her for that.

When I got closer, I slowed down and tried to be stealthy. I didn't want her to realize I was there until I could assess the situation. I began to creep closer to the dilapidated little structure. It had really deteriorated since I had been there last. It was actually leaning to one side and a lot of the boards and logs were missing. The front porch was being held up by several boards that were propped against it. The windows that hadn't been broken out back then, were blasted out with bits of glass mingled in with the dirt below the windows. There was no light on inside and I began to wonder if this was some sort of trick.

I slowly made my way towards the back of the cabin when chaos erupted. The big burly guys from the Volvo suddenly surrounded me and two of them were pinning my arms down at my sides with grips of steel. I tried thrashing around but that only resulted in burly guy #3 grabbing my legs before I could kick him where I intended. Lindsey appeared out of nowhere and had a look of pity on her face. If I had the use of my hands, I would have gladly and forcibly wiped the look off with my fists.

"There is no reason to be upset, Phoebe. This had to be done and no one here wants to harm you."

"You could have fooled me." I gestured with my head to the guys holding me captive.

"There would be no need for that if you just agree to listen to what we have to say."

I gave her a look that warned her that we would not be agreeing on anything this night. She gestured to the guys to place me in an SUV that I didn't even see sitting around the side of the cabin.

"Where are you taking me and where is Bob?"

"Bob is fine. I never even took him. I just said that because I knew you would come right away and I was right." She smirked at me like we were still best friends. I knew that if I had my hands released I would easily throw my blue fire at her without any remorse.

The men placed me in the SUV and continued to hold me down even after they buckled me in. I felt like I couldn't breathe, I was so angry with her. She was consorting with the people who were after me and I would never forgive her. I had no idea where we were going and I vowed to watch for every road sign and landmark so I could find my way back right before they put a black hood over my face that blocked out absolutely everything. I tried to get away but it was no use.

After what seemed like forever on the road, but was probably realistically closer to half an hour, the SUV stopped and the men were unbuckling me and yanking me out, being careful to keep my arms pinned so I couldn't harm anyone. I was dragged unceremoniously across gravel. I could hear it crunching under my feet as I tried to walk but my captors continued pulling me along. I could hear a door creek open and close with a resounding thud. My hood was finally removed and I took a moment just to breathe normally without the cloth restricting my lungs. It took several moments for my eyes to adjust to the light. My hands were still pinned down and I was standing in an enormous foyer. The floors were made of wood and polished until they gleamed with a light of their own. There was a large chandelier illuminating the space and the crystals that hung from it were captivating. Ahead of me was a winding staircase and off to each side were rooms that I could not see into because the doors were closed. Under any other circumstances, I would have been impressed with my surroundings.

Lindsey appeared in front of me and was sure my eyes were burning holes through her face. She just looked at me with a smile on her face like we were playing a fun game of hide and seek and she had just found me hiding in a coat closet. She knew she had the upper hand, but I knew it would not always be that way. I hoped she could see the retribution that I promised burning into her soul.

"I know you're angry Phoebe but there is no need to be. You are about to meet your real dad. He is so excited to see you!" As she said this her voice increased with a glee that I could not share. Her eyes shined like she had just won the Pulitzer Prize and was ready to give her acceptance speech. She looked at me waiting for some sort of reaction and I refused to give her one.

She grimaced at my resistance and gestured to the men to bring me into a room that was located off to my left. "You will thank me later Phoebe. I will be waiting for it."

They led me into a room that looked like an old-fashioned sitting room. There were settees and overstuffed chairs dispersed around the room. The walls were painted a cheery yellow and there were three large windows with beautiful yellow and white draperies that hung to the ground. The windows afforded the room a lot of natural light and lended itself to the cheerful appeal. Under any other circumstance I would have admired it. Right now, the only thing I wanted to do was knock my chair over, hit the men with my blue fire and search for Lindsey and make her pay.

I was lost in thoughts of my escape when an older man walked into the room. He looked to be in his forties and he walked with an air of distinction. He had hair that was graying at the temples and wore a navy blue polo shirt and black trousers. He was about five foot eleven and wore black designer shoes. He stopped a few feet in front of me and looked at me with tears clouding his eyes.

"Unhand her. That is my daughter. Get out of the room!"

The men that had been pinning my arms down got up quickly and practically ran out of the room. It was obvious this man in front of me had all the power. I considered throwing my blue fire at him but my curiosity got the better of me.

"Who are you and why was I dragged here?" I asked as I kneaded my sore arms.

He leaned down and took both of my hands in his raising me from the chair. When I was standing up, he didn't let go of my hands as he looked me up and down. "Phoebe, I am your dad. I have waited a lifetime to meet you!" With that, he enveloped me in a hug and I could hear his muffled sobs. When he finally let go he took out a handkerchief and dabbed at his eyes. "Please sit down. I am so sorry about the manner in which you were transported here. It is unseemly. I told Lindsey to extend an invitation to you and instead of telling me you had declined, she took matters into her own hands and for that I am deeply apologetic."

He sat down in the overstuffed chair across from me. I didn't see any resemblance between him and I. He had dark brown eyes and a long aristocratic nose. He was slender and sophisticated, not the type of man I could picture my mom falling for. She always said that she preferred people that were down to earth and always acted like themselves and he didn't seem to fit that profile in the least.

"You must have a million questions for me. I will be very transparent and honest and tell you anything you want to know."

It almost seemed as if he could read my mind and considering there was a possibility he had abilities, I needed to proceed with caution. "I don't see any resemblance between you and I, no offense. I also can't picture my mom with someone like you. You're going to have to do a lot of convincing if you think that I am just going to believe you because you seem to be happy to see me."

He didn't look the least bit taken aback by my statements, almost like he was expecting me to say that. "I see your mother in you. You're right, I don't see a lot of physical resemblance between us but that doesn't make me any less your father. Your mother and I met a long time ago. She was in college and just coming into her powers. She was magnificent and beautiful. I thought I wouldn't have a chance with her but I wore her down. I just kept asking her out until she finally relented. I sometimes think she did it so I would stop asking." He chuckled a bit and seemed to look into the distance caught in a memory.

I took her skydiving on our first date and she was hooked ever since. She and I were inseparable, we loved taking risks but we always took them together. I called her my little firecracker." He laughed nostalgically.

"When she graduated from college, we started talking about a future together. I loved her more than anything in this world and I thought she loved me the same way. One day, she just left. She left behind this note and it baffled me until the day I realized we had gotten pregnant then it all made sense. By then it was too late and she was gone." He handed me the note and dabbed at his eyes again with his handkerchief.

My Dearest Julian,

I am so sorry to leave this way but I fear it is the only way I will be able to do it. If I explain myself in person, I know that I will be swayed to stay and I can't do that. I do love you and probably always will but we can't be together. There is no future in it, and I have come to realize that lately. I know that we talked of a future but whenever we do it is always about you and I and all the adventurous things we can do together. There is never any mention of settling down and having children and I know now that is what I want most of all. It is that missing piece of my life that I never realized was missing until recently. Don't try to look for me, it won't change anything for us. This is goodbye.

Love Always,

Anna

I didn't realize I was crying until one of the tears dripped onto the eloquently written letter. I quickly brushed it off so I didn't ruin his letter. That was definitely my mom's handwriting.

"So, how do you know she was pregnant with me when she left? How do you know I am yours and not the man who raised me? I was told Crissnas could not reproduce in that way."

"It is impossible for you to be Bob's daughter as he is completely human and you are a hybrid. Your mom was a Vampire and I am a hybrid, and the dates match up of when we were together. Bob had to know that he wasn't yours. I understand he was not a very loving substitute father and for that I am so very sorry. If I had known that she was carrying our child, I would have searched to the ends of the earth to find her. When I got this letter, I was heartbroken and too proud to look for her." He paused for a moment seeming to collect his thoughts.

" She broke me and it took a long time for me to get back to myself and even then I was never the same. I never married or had a family. She was always that missing part of my heart and now I have no way of telling her that or letting her know just how much she meant to me. But I do have you and I will cherish you for the rest of time. I have so much to share with you and so much to tell you. I want to keep you safe so please consider yourself a guest here. I have an entire wing of rooms that I have decorated for you and they are all yours. You can have as much privacy as you want but I hope that you will carve out time to talk to me and spend time with me"

"Woah, wait just a minute. I have a home and a life. I appreciate that you want to get to know me and all but it will have to be on my terms. I am not ready to give up my life and my home to get to know you." I couldn't even believe that he would think that I would do such a thing. Seriously, how could he think I would even consider it?

His demeanor seemed to change at my confession. He stood up and loomed over me for a moment before he regained his composure. He stepped back and gave me a little space, which is good, because I was considering defending myself as I still was not one hundred percent convinced that this was for real. "I know this is all a great shock for you. I understand also the way you were brought here was less than ideal, but please consider my generous offer. You would not want for anything, you would not have to work so it would give you plenty of time to finish your novel. I am also protecting you from the Vampire family that you have cleaved to for too long. They are not your family, I am and I don't know what lies they are telling you but you are a hybrid and I am here to take care of you, not them."

"They are not liars. I have become very close with them and right now I consider them more family than I can consider you. I just met you and I am still not completely convinced. I would like to get to know you but you need to understand that I have a job, a life, and a home that I am not willing to sacrifice. You also have still not answered my question about how a Vampire and a Crissna could have a child."

My head was buzzing with everything I had just learned and everything that I was supposed to just accept. I was not a pawn in some game that he could manipulate around on a chess board. He needed to give me some space and being in the same home right now was not enough space for me. I needed to get back before Alaric and Xander went out of their minds wondering where I was. I couldn't hurt them like that.

For a moment, the look on his face was determined and hard and I wondered if he was going to try to keep me here regardless of my wishes to leave. The expression disappeared and in its place, he seemed disappointed and downcast. "I had hoped that we would have more time to get to know one another and that you would stay but I should have been more realistic. I don't want to push you to do anything you are not ready for but I hope that you will allow me to come and visit you. I am sorry that we have kept the location a secret from you and unfortunately we will have to do that again because at this time, it isn't safe for anyone to know where I am. I will be in touch with you and we can arrange to meet. I really loved your mother and I regret that I did not get to see you grow up. I want a chance to know my daughter, please."

There were so many things I wanted to say and ask. *Why was this location private? If he really considered me his daughter and wanted to get to know me, why couldn't he trust me? He hadn't really told me anything about himself and it seemed like the conversation was coming to an end.* In the end, I didn't give voice to any of that because he seemed so downtrodden because I had refused his offer.

"I hope that we will get to know each other."

He walked toward me as if to embrace me then took a step back and turned around and walked to the doors. "Please escort my daughter home and find a better blind fold. I don't want a damn hood over her head all the way there. Treat her with the respect she deserves." He turned around with one last look at me and walked away. It was kind of anticlimactic after everything I had been through in the last few hours. The skeptic in me couldn't help but wonder what he was really up to. I didn't trust him, I still wasn't sure he was my father, he didn't seem to want to share any information with me except how he met my mom, and he was being enigmatic about how we would meet again. He had also known about the hood and the unceremonious way I was brought to him. If he didn't have anything to do with that, then how did he have so much knowledge about it when I had just entered his home. I had every reason to distrust him.

Lindsey walked back into the room and strode toward me like we were still best friends. "Hey girl, I am glad that is all worked out. You finally got to meet your dad! I am so excited for you. Are you staying here?"

The men at the door explained that they were taking me home and she looked like they had slapped her in the face with a wet towel. She looked at me like she could not believe I was not taking this opportunity that was presented to me. I wanted to smack her into next week. Instead, I ignored her and turned to the men that had abducted me. "Please take me home now."

As I began walking out with them, she grabbed me by the arm and spun me around. "You're serious right now? You're not even going to say goodbye to me or thank me for bringing you to your dad?"

"Of course, what was I thinking? Let me just give you my best thank you." I said as I walked right up to her and gave her my best left hook right in her face. I didn't realize just how much strength I had until she fell and skidded right across the smooth floors into the not so smooth wall. Her head crashed through the plaster making a head-sized hole. She looked dazed and I didn't wait around to see what her rebuttal would be. I turned around and sauntered to the door, begrudgingly taking the blindfold I was offered and placing it across my eyes. The men walked me to the SUV and helped me get inside the back seat. I could tell I was placed in the middle because I could feel them get in on each side of me. Apparently, dear old dad didn't trust me too much. I remained silent on the way back and so did they and I preferred it that way. When the SUV stopped, I could hear the doors opening and I was praying that I was home and Alaric and Xander weren't too frantic yet. One of the burly men took off my blindfold and I realized I was back at the cabin.

"You will have to walk from here." Without another word, he turned around and got back into the SUV and they were off. Great, the first rays of sunshine began making their debut in the sky, so I was going to have to be careful about my speed. I couldn't exactly run like I did to get here, too much of a chance of being seen. Ugh! All I wanted to do was get home and reassure everyone I was ok and get some rest. I felt overwhelmed and exhausted.

I walked as quickly as I could and when I sensed no one was around, I ran for part of the trek. I finally arrived at home only to find the entire family there. Alaric was the first one to get to me. He grabbed me and held on, swinging me around in his arms. When I finally got a glimpse of his face, it looked like he had aged a thousand years in one night. There were worry lines around his eyes and he looked like he had been continuously running his hands through his hair like he does when he is stressed. He had unshed tears in his eyes and at the sight of those, I couldn't help but kiss him to reassure him that I was ok. I completely forgot about our audience and if that kiss was any indication so did Alaric. When we finally took a breath and broke apart everyone was gathered around us. His mom and dad were actually beaming at us, Alyssa was jumping up and down with excitement, and Xander looked like he had just been hit by a brick.

"I knew you would be ok. I am so happy that you and Alaric are together!" Alyssa squealed. She hugged us both and then resumed jumping up and down. She looked over and realized Xander was upset and gave him a hug and held onto him. They spoke softly to each other and

I was trying to hear what they were saying when their mom and dad swooped in for hugs.

"I know you have been through something and we need to go in and talk about it, but I want you to know that I am so grateful you are back and ok and that you and our son are together. We have begun to love you like family and soon you will be. We couldn't be more ecstatic." Belle said as she hugged me tight.

"Thank you. I am very lucky to have all of you."

Steven came in for a hug and suggested we all go inside and talk about what happened.

Once everyone was in my suddenly too small living room, I brought in the chairs from the kitchen so everyone would have some place to sit. I let his mom and dad sit on the couch while the rest of us occupied the chairs and the carpeted floor. They all looked at me expectantly and I knew I could not put off telling them where I had been. I took a deep breath to try to clear my head before I began.

"I first want to apologize for worrying everyone. I never would have left without a word if I didn't think someone was in danger. I got a text from Lindsey late last night and she stated that she had Bob, the man who helped to raise me. She said if I came to the cabin where we used to hang out when we were teens, that she would let him go but she needed to talk to me. She cautioned me that if I alerted anyone, he would be harmed."

I looked down and took another breath. The guilt over everything was swelling up inside my chest. I felt equal amounts nauseous and defeated.

"Go on Phoebe, we all know how kind you are and that you would never allow anything to happen to anyone you know. No one here is going to hold that against you. Please tell us what happened." Xander stated as he looked at me like he wanted to hold me. That just about broke me because I knew how hard it was for him to see Alaric and I together. I nodded and smiled at him and pushed on with my story.

"When I got there, they ambushed me. Lindsey was there with the guys from the Volvo that we scared away that night. Bob wasn't even with them. They had never taken him in the first place, she used that as a ploy to get me there. Anyway, they shoved me into an SUV and put a hood over my head." I started to hear sympathetic sounds from his family and Alaric held my hand tighter as we sat there. He looked at me and nodded telling me through his mind that he loves me and to keep going at my pace.

"They brought me to this huge home and introduced me to a man that claims to be my father. He claims that he is a hybrid and that I am too."

"Do you believe him?" asked Steven.

"He showed me a note that my mother had written to him before I was born, breaking off their relationship because she wanted to have a family and he didn't. He said that she never told him she was pregnant with me when she left but that the dates match up and I have to be his. I just didn't think Crissnas could have children and he never answered my question about how that was possible."

I think in the back of my mind, I wanted to hear them all tell me that it wasn't possible but they all just sat silently waiting for me to continue my story.

"He really didn't give me much information about himself, except that his name is Julian, and he said he loved my mom. He tried to get me to stay there and even fixed up an entire wing of his house for me. For a while, I felt like he was going to keep me there against my will but he let me go. The men that abducted me took me back to the cabin and I walked from there."

Alaric scooted his chair even closer so he could hold me instead of just holding my hand. He was my rock and I felt the strength from his body seeping into mine, giving me the motivation to be able to get through all of this.

Steven spoke first. "I know you said you were unable to see. Do you think there is any way you might be able to identify where you were being held?"

I described the interior of the home in great detail to them and the fact that we were probably only traveling for about a half hour.

"We might be able to narrow down a search trajectory. Did he give you any contact information?" asked Steven.

"No. He said he would be in contact with me in order to visit with me more to get to know each other. I don't know if he is my real dad or not, but I didn't get a very good feeling being there. He seemed apologetic about the means of getting me there but only in words. There was no sentiment behind it."

"Well, if he gets in contact with you at any time please let one of us know. No matter what he or Lindsey or anyone threatens from now on, you need to let us help you. That is what family is for and we would never let anything happen to you."

"I know and I am sorry. I have been doing everything myself for what seems like my entire life, that it was almost natural for me to try to take care of this myself. I should have involved you all and I really do apologize. I won't make you all worry like that again."

They all nodded and looked sympathetic, even Xander. Alaric gave me a squeeze and kissed my forehead. This was both strange and wonderful to have this family who cared so much for me. I was truly blessed. My anxiety just melted away and in its place was this reassurance that they would always be there for me.

"Wait, I think we were all focusing on what happened to you and where you were and missed a part of your story." Belle stated. "Did you say something about Julian stating that you are a hybrid?"

"Yes, I know I am new to all of this, but I don't remember any of you telling me about hybrids."

"That is because we didn't. They have always been more of a myth. No one really thought they could be real since the way Vampires and Crissnas are created are as different as night and day. Did he explain it any further?"

"No, he just stated it like it was an everyday fact. My mom was a Vampire and he is a Crissna so he stated that I am a hybrid like it was no big deal."

The entire family looked around at one another like I had sprouted a third arm. Muy anxiety returned in full force.

"I will try to find out more about all of this. If hybrids do exist and you are one we will seek out as much information as we can for you. In the meantime, I think we need to come up with a new plan for protecting you. No one knows what this Julian is going to do from here and I think you were lucky not to be harmed this time. There is a possibility he could be your dad but we are going to err on the side of caution and protect you from him for now until we have more information. How would you feel about staying with us?"

When I looked shell shocked he went on. " I know that you value your independence and I appreciate that but I also know that we can't keep you safe here unless we all move in with you and we would all be more comfortable at our home. Your place is beautiful but we would all be tripping over each other here." Steven said with a chuckle.

I knew that he was right but it was still hard to know that I was going to have to leave my perfect little home. I loved this place and who knew how long this would take. The idea of being around Alaric all the time gave me a little incentive though. *"You can stay in my room."* Alaric said through our connection. I was sure I was blushing when I looked up and accepted Steven's invitation.

"I appreciate all of you and everything you are doing for me." I said as I looked around at each of them and smiled. "I am going to have to gather some of my things before we leave."

"Of course, do you want my help?" asked Alyssa as she bounced over to me as I stood up.

"Sure, of course. Thank you." She just hugged me and we walked into the bedroom to gather up clothes. I would need to bring both my suitcases for my clothes and all my makeup and toiletries.

" I know how independent you are and this is going to be a change but you are going to love living with us. I promise." She hugged me tight and once I had everything I needed, we went back to join the others. This really wasn't the worst thing to ever happen to me and there were perks like getting to know the family better and spending more time with Alaric. I told myself this was for the best and I would be excited about it.

We all loaded into our vehicles and I took one last long look at my home. It was bittersweet leaving, and I had this feeling that I wouldn't be seeing it for a long time. It was just this nagging feeling in the back of my mind and it left me emotional, like I had something lodged in my throat and the tears threatened to appear. I pushed them back, telling myself this was the right direction to take. I got into my car with Alaric by my side and I refused to look in the rear view mirror. My new life was ahead of me, not behind and even though Julian and Lindsey weren't there to see it, I didn't want to give them the satisfaction of knowing I was worried about my future because of them.

Chapter Nine

A New Atmosphere

I settled in pretty quickly at my new temporary or maybe more permanent home. It was decided that I would stay with Alaric, it was obvious to everyone that was where I belonged and I was surprised not to have any reaction from Xander so I readily agreed. I always felt safe and loved with Alaric so I was content to be with him as much as possible.

I took a leave of absence from work so I had time to get through all of this. I had to lie to my boss and tell him I had a family emergency but he was surprisingly supportive and told me to take all the time I needed. I felt awful being untruthful with him. I hated being lied to and here I was doing the thing I loathed most.

During the days, I spent time working on my abilities and realized I could also read thoughts from anyone if I concentrated enough. Each of my other abilities were almost perfected and I could call on them without thought.

When I wasn't with Alaric, I spent a lot of time with Alyssa. She was like the sister I always wanted but never had. We had so much in common and her bubbly spirit and tenacity was starting to rub off on me and I was feeling a lot lighter these days.

Xander helped me to hone my abilities and even though I would catch him staring at me longingly at times, it was mostly platonic. I knew that he wanted me to feel at home and that his part in that was giving up any idea of a romance between us. I was sure he could see the growing love between Alaric and I so he knew when to back off. I know we all still had the dreams and I was hoping that now that things were mostly settled between all of us that those would cease but they continued.

Steven and Belle continued to make me feel at home. Steven was everything I wish my dad Bob could have been while I was growing up. Where Bob lacked compassion, Steven had a copious amount to give willingly. Bob would always look at me with a coldness in his heart that showed in his expression. Steven looked at me with love, like I was a daughter to him just as much as Alyssa was.

Belle was wonderful and reminded me so much of my own mom that sometimes it made me equal amounts sad and thrilled. She was so nurturing and she seemed to pick up on my moods even faster than Alaric and she was always there to lend an ear or provide a shoulder for me. I loved her to pieces and I couldn't imagine my life without her or any of them in it anymore.

I still got texts from Lindsey from time to time asking me for forgiveness or telling me just how much she missed me. She would sometimes tell me that Julian wanted to meet with me but I wasn't ready for that yet even though I had told him I would try to get to know him. So, her texts went unanswered but that never made her give up.

My evenings were spent on skill perfection some nights and other nights we just all spent time together as a family. We did normal family things like game night and watching movies together. We were a family of Vampires, it was still weird to think that way, but that is what we were.

The nights spent with Alaric were electric, there were no words to accurately describe them.   At first, I felt very intimidated by the fact that the rest of his family was under the same roof. I didn't want them to think badly of me because of the things Alaric and I were doing together. I especially wondered about Xander and his feelings about Alaric and I sharing a bed.

It didn't take long for Alaric to break down those walls for me. "My family all knows that we are together and in this family that means forever. For me, this is forever. I never want to lose you and you are right where you are supposed to be. When I started having the dreams about you, after waiting for so many years to find my love, it was difficult for me to accept. I don't know why, I guess it was a shock to know that you may one day be mine. I think I fell in love with you before I even met you. I would watch you and you always had such a kind heart. Even when your mom passed, I would watch you trying to be there for others and comfort them by putting your own feelings of loss aside. . You always thought of yourself last, and that is a rare trait. I saw you when your friend lost her dad and you were there for her and helped her through. I bet you didn't know that she had considered suicide before you began helping her. If it weren't for your kindness, she may not be here today. When Xander began having the dreams as well and we realized they were about you, I was so confused and angry. I couldn't imagine being ripped away from you, the very thought of it made me physically ill. I was willing to stand aside though if Xander ended up being the one for you, the one to make you happy. All I ever want is your happiness."

Those statements alone nearly broke me. How could anyone love me as much as I love them? It was unfathomable to me. I was nothing special, no one special. I always felt like Alaric had more to offer me than I had to offer him. I had grown up with my mom loving me, my dad at the least being ambivalent about me at worst hating me, and a few friends, one who ended up being the biggest liar and fake there ever was. I sometimes felt like I was inside some kind of fairy tale and I was going to wake up to find my normal and bleak life, spending the rest of it trying to find the dream that I had lost.

Every look, every touch from Alaric was a gift and I wanted to do everything in my power to keep on deserving those gifts. I loved him so much that at times, I felt that I would burst with my emotions.

I spent my nights with him after that talk, even though I know that was not his goal by telling me everything that he did. Every time he wrapped his arms around me, I felt his strength seeping into me. His mind was filled with love for me and there was no denying my love for him. The nights were exquisite. Just when I thought it couldn't get any better, he found different ways to bring me to the edge and back again. I would never grow tired of this. I am not sure even an eternity was enough time for his love and the way he made me feel.

Months went by and there was less and less communication with the outside world. I still enjoyed working on my book in my down time, which was understandably less than it used to be. I was just getting used to my new life, my new powers, and I was just getting comfortable when it all began to change.

Chapter Ten

The Change

I was outside one morning, enjoying my coffee, when I received a text that ended up ultimately changing my life.

"I need to see you right away. I am utilizing Lindsey's phone but this is your father Julian. Crissnas have begun to get wind of you and I have been doing everything in my power to keep them at bay but I am afraid that they will be coming for you soon. I never explained my importance in this world to you and I should have. I was remiss and for that I sincerely apologize. I need to explain the danger you are in and find some way to get you out of it. Please respond to this text. I will meet you at your home, your former address after dark. Please heed this warning. I need to help you."

Well, damn. I knew that something would eventually happen when I continued to ignore Lindsey and her constant texts and attempted calls, but I wasn't prepared for that. Was this another one of his setups and the Arnold Schwarzenegger look-alikes would be waiting for me again to whisk me away to dear old dad's house? I was not going to be caught unaware this time. I was more prepared. My powers were a lot stronger than they were the last time we met and even pinning down my arms was not going to keep me from fighting.

My sense of panic must have sprung Alaric into action because he was beside me asking what was going on before I had time to contemplate it myself. I explained what was happening. His voice was calm and I knew he was calculating all the risks.

"We will talk to the family and we will help you to make a decision about what to do. I don't want Julian or Lindsey to get the bright idea to try to get someone to cause problems for you before we have a chance to work this out. Ok?"

"I feel better already."

"That is perfect. I love you."

"I love you too."I never got tired of hearing that from him and I was sure I never would. We sat there for a while waiting for everyone else to start their day so we could figure this out. He held me close and we sat in silence just soaking up our time together. The birds had begun their morning songs and the woods were alive with other animals out hunting for their breakfast. The sun was peeking through the trees creating a halo around our home. That was when I realized I really was home. I was surrounded by those that loved me as much as I adored them. We were all here for each other in good times and bad. My heart spilled over with gratitude that they were a part of my life.

Chapter Eleven

What is Next?

Alaric took my hand on the way into the house, and an instant calm overtook me. I was so grateful for his tranquil effect on my fluttering heart. Sometimes he was like a drug to me. I craved him in so many ways. I never knew that love could be all consuming, probably because I hadn't had much experience with it. I never really saw a great love between my parents and I was picky about men so I had never had a great love until now.

When we reached the french doors that led inside, he gathered me into his arms and kissed me with abandon and then ushered me in. I felt weightless and electrified at the same time. I wasn't sure what I had done to deserve this amazing man, but I felt like the luckiest person in the world.

As we waited for everyone to gather in the family room, I tried to imagine what Julian wanted. I still felt like something was off with him. The last time I saw him, I hadn't discovered my power to hear people's thoughts so maybe this was a good thing. Maybe this time, I would be able to read his thoughts and really figure out what he was up to. I wanted to think that he was just my father and wanted to get to know me, but I was not the same naive girl I was months ago before I found out about my real life and my true identity.

Steven and Belle had continued to look into Julian but they kept coming up with dead ends. It was the same with why I had more than one active power, they could not figure out why. They had tried every avenue and they would continue to work on it, but so far nothing. I was some kind of anomaly. The only thing that they had figured out with some certainty is that hybrids do not exist. So that really made Lindsey and Julian even more suspect since they claimed that she and I are hybrids. None of us could figure out their angle, but maybe this evening we would finally get our chance.

Alaric sensed my unease and kissed me softly at first but the kiss soon became an inferno. It stopped too soon when Alyssa cleared her throat. "I'm sorry you two, but everyone else is headed in." She looked so apologetic, I couldn't be upset with her. Alaric put his hand on the small of my back to guide me to a seat and Alyssa held my hand and we walked.

The atmosphere was all business and you could cut the tension with a knife. I suddenly felt like there wasn't enough air in the room. I sat down with Alaric and waited for someone to say something but they were all looking at me. I purposefully didn't read any thoughts because I was afraid of what I would hear. Alaric explained about the text and we all waited.

Finally, Steven broke the silence. "I think I speak for everyone when I say we are all concerned about tonight. We understand that this is something you have to do. It is inevitable to meet with Julian or we feel he will start taking more drastic measures to see you and none of us wants that. Julian wants you to come alone and that is going to be the difficult part. None of us wants to leave you alone with him, because until he proves that he can be trusted, we won't trust him."

By this time, every nerve ending in my body was on high alert and I was beginning to become even more anxious and I didn't think that was possible. I looked around the room at everyone and they all had the same tense look on their faces except for Alaric who looked like he just wanted to take me to his room and never let me out.

"Ok, what do you need me to do?"

"We are going to form a perimeter about a mile out in all directions. We will stay back but we can get there quickly if anything goes wrong." declared Steven.

"No way! She is not getting out of my sight. I don't care if Julian wants her there alone or not. She is my life now and there is no separating us for any reason." stated Alaric as he squeezed my hand.

"We had a feeling you would say that but your bond is too strong and they may sense you if you try to stay too close to her. We are going to send Xander just a few steps behind her. They will have less chance of detecting him. He will stay hidden in the car if she needs help. We will all be close enough without being detected to help too, including you." Steven said. Belle looked on with a sympathetic look and placed her comforting hand on his shoulder.

"I know that if it were your dad out there, I would want to be the one right next to him to keep him safe. I get it. We just feel that your connection is so strong they will sense it and he will go running. We need to know what Julian is up to and so far we haven't been successful in obtaining any information. This may help and if we know he has an his agenda, then we can help Phoebe more effectively."

That seemed to placate Alaric but my head was doing a tail spin. So many things could go wrong. I had to try to think positive, for my sake and Alaric's. I needed to keep my head straight and figure out what Julian was up to. I smiled up at Alaric and tried to keep my mind clear of all the confusion so he didn't stop me from leaving. I needed to get this over with.

After some more strategizing, we were as ready as we could be. Everyone except Xander had to leave first to set the perimeter before Xander and I headed out to meet Julian. Belle and Alyssa hugged me and told me they would see me soon. Steven just gave me an encouraging nod, which left just one person to say goodbye to. Alaric stood in front of me with his heart on his sleeve. I could tell by the intensity of his eyes that he didn't want to leave. I knew it was up to me to convince him that it would be ok and I would see him soon. I lifted myself onto my tiptoes and brushed my lips softly across his. I could hear his sudden intake of breath as he reached out and pulled me possessively to him. There wasn't an inch of room between us and it was hard to tell where he ended and I began. I could feel the tension of the evening uncoiling in my core as a different type of tension built up inside me. He leaned in and intensified the kiss. I wrapped my arms around him and held on like he was my lifeline. I momentarily forgot about the mission that I needed to complete as he was suddenly my everything.

He ended the kiss and brought his forehead to mine. "This thing with Julian will get figured out. Once the danger is over, we can be together forever. I never want to lose you."

He turned to Xander, "Don't let anything happen to her please."

Xander replied, "You know that I will guard her with my life. If anything untoward happens, I will be out of that car in less than a second. I am not going to let Julian or anyone do anything to her."

Alaric looked at me one last time and headed out. Xander and I waited for about ten minutes then we got into the car and began to go to the cabin. He laid down in the back seat so Julian and whoever was with Julian wouldn't detect him. I was really hopeful that we would find out some intel at this meeting. I wanted to stop hiding and feeling like a rabbit being chased by a coyote.

I was tired of always looking over my shoulder and being confined to the house.

Chapter Twelve

The Beginning of Hell

I rolled up to the cabin, but not too close so that no one would see Xander. I didn't look in the back as I slowly got out of the car. The world was encased in gloom like a sticky ink that wouldn't wash out. The air was heavy and felt like it weighed me down as I walked. My feet scrunched on the ground as I got closer to the cabin. I saw Julian walk around from the back alone.

"Ah, daughter, come closer so that I can see you. How I have missed you!"

I couldn't help but feel like Little Red Riding Hood as the wolf disguised as her grandmother beckoned her forward. I walked a little closer and let him bridge the rest of the distance. His eyes seemed too bright, too welcoming and I was afraid this was a facade. He embraced me awkwardly and I felt entombed in his arms, not the way a daughter should feel about her dad. I just knew in my gut that he couldn't be trusted.

"Why has it taken you so long to come and see me? Have I done something to offend you? I told you the first time we met that I just want to get to know you and it feels like you are denying me that privilege."

"I would like to remind you of how you invited me to your home last time, a little less than hospitable. I am wary of you, Julian. It seems like you are too eager to get me on my own. I don't know why you objected to allowing me to bring Alaric with me. If you really want to get to know me then you should be willing to get to know him too since he is a permanent fixture in my life."

He looked astonished that I was the least bit angry with him. He opened his eyes widely like none of this had ever occurred to him before. "Well, of course next time we meet, feel free to bring Alaric along with you. I didn't realize it was that serious between the two of you.".

"I recall you telling me not to trust anyone in that family."

"Surely you misunderstood." He looked at me like one would a child who is too young to know right from wrong. He was already getting under my skin. Surely my mom was never in love with him. Ugh.

He looked around like he was watching for something out in the distance and the hairs on the back of my neck stood at attention. My muscles tensed up ready for a fight. My head whipped around and all I saw was darkness, nothing creeping around me. My attention returned to Julian, but my senses were still on alert. I could feel the adrenaline coursing through my veins.

He put a serene expression on his face which I was starting to learn meant trouble. "Why don't we take a little stroll, talk, and get to know each other? I am so interested in how you are doing."

He started to pull me towards him with his left arm nearing my shoulder. I tried to back away and he nodded off to his right. I slipped under his arm as I backed away and looked in the direction of his nod but too late. Something hard had crashed over my head. As I melted to the ground, I could feel the warmth from my blood trickling down my face and in front of my eyes. My last thought was that I would never see Alaric again.

Chapter Thirteen

The Depths of Hell

I woke up in total darkness. I tried to sit up and the world swam in circles around me so I laid my head back down. I was lying on what felt like a cloud, it was so soft and warm. It took my eyes a moment to adjust to the lack of light. I was lying on a huge four poster bed in a room that was as large as my entire little house. There was an old fashioned trunk at the end of the bed and a wardrobe across the room. There were two doors and I needed to find out where they led. It took a few minutes for the dizziness to pass. I grabbed my head and felt the dried blood but there wasn't any soreness, which kind of surprised me. *How long had I been out and where the hell was I?*

I got up soundlessly and walked to the first door. When I opened it and found the light switch, before me was an opulent bathroom. There was a claw foot tub large enough for four people, a shower that had several shower heads with different settings, and a double sink with marble inlay. There were delicate looking towels by the sink and little varieties of soaps. It was the most beautiful bathroom I had ever seen, as bathrooms go. I wanted to go in and wash the blood off of my head but I needed to find a way out of there. I turned off the light and shut the door quietly. I crept over to the other door that would hopefully lead to my freedom.

I opened the door inch by inch. I could feel my heart beating rapidly in my chest and my breath was coming out in quick pants. All I could think about was getting out and making sure my family was ok. The thought of them being my family was new and created a smile across my face, despite my circumstances. As I made it past the door, the winding and dark hallway greeted me like a ghost in the night. Not another being could be seen or heard and while I took that as a good thing, it also made me wary. I reached the top of the winding staircase and realized I was in Julian's home. I had already surmised as much, but now I had confirmation.

It surprised me that no one was guarding my door or the stairs and trying to stop me, since they went to all the trouble to get me there in the first place. I made it all the way downstairs and was halfway to the door when his voice stopped me in my tracks.

"I see you are awake. Where do you think you are going?" Julian asked in a voice that just made me cringe. I debated trying to race him to the door or throwing my blue fire at him. Instead, I turned slowly around and marched straight for him.

"Who the hell do you think you are? I met with you in good faith to try to have some kind of relationship with you and you thank me by knocking me out and kidnapping me?" I said all this while poking my finger into his chest. "If you think for one second that I am going to sit here and allow this to happen, you don't know me at all. You can take your father-daughter relationship and stick it up your ass."

With that, I turned on my heel and raced to the door. He made no move to stop me but suddenly there was a blood sucker blocking the door. I raised my arm and threw my blue fire at him. He lit up like he was being electrocuted and then burst into flames. He started to run toward me screeching like a little girl when he turned to ash. I headed back to the door when I heard some rustling behind me and what Julian said next made me screech to a halt.

"You're not going to go and leave Xander behind, are you?"

"What the...." I said as I turned and that is when I saw him. His arms were bound and the guard standing behind him holding him looked like he wanted to do nothing more than cut off his head with the very large and menacing knife he held against Xander's throat. Xander looked like he had been in a bar fight and got the wind knocked out of him. He was slightly hunched forward. He mouthed to me to just go. I knew I could never leave him behind.

"Stop, let him go now." I started to raise my arms.

"Just so you know Phoebe, if you do what I think you are about to do, the next breath Xander takes will be his very last."

I weighed my options. I could send my blue fire at Julian but I couldn't send it to him and all the guards at the same time. I began to read Julian's mind and he had every intention of following through on his threat. I considered leaving when I read Xander's mind and he was telling me over and over to leave while I could. He would be ok. I considered it for a split second, but I could never hurt Xander. He had been nothing but kind to me, despite the fact that I had rejected him and not only that, chosen his brother. I couldn't hurt him even more by leaving him to Julian and his brigade of monsters. They would not bother to keep him alive if I left.

"Let him go Julian and I will stay. Xander has nothing to do with any of this." At this point, I was equal parts scared for Xander and pissed off that Julian had gotten away with taking us both. I wanted to kill him, all I needed was a plan.

"No, I don't think I will do that. He will be my *guest* for now. I need your compliance Phoebe and if I have to use Xander in order to get it then I will." He nodded to Xander's guard and the guard started leading Xander further into the house.

"Where are you taking him?""He will be here in his own quarters. You will have your room which I assume you found to your liking. Once we get to know each other better, and I know that I can trust you then you will be able to see Xander again.""How do I know you're not going to hurt him? I demand that you let him go or I will..."

"Tsk, tsk, you are in no position to *demand* anything from me. You go back up to your room. Wash off all of that blood and try to look presentable. You have my word that no harm will come to Xander as long as you are abiding by my house rules."

I felt the fire burning just under my skin. I wanted nothing more than to rid myself of Julian and all of his henchmen but I knew I would need to bide my time. I needed to get Julian to trust me just enough so that I could get Xander safely out of here and hopefully save myself in the process. I couldn't imagine the fear that the rest of the family had. I couldn't imagine how Alaric must be feeling to lose me and his brother in one night and have no idea where to look for us. I gave Julain one more defiant look and trudged up the stairs feeling utterly defeated.

When I got up to my room, I went straight for the bathroom. I couldn't wait to wash all of the blood off of myself and feel clean again. I pulled out a towel and jumped into the shower. All the showerheads made it feel like I was getting a shower and a back massage in one. It felt terrible to indulge but after what I had been through I needed a minute to get my head clear so I could further formulate my plan to get out of there with Xander.

When I was finished, and I finally felt clean, I got out and wrapped myself in a towel and grabbed the robe that I assumed was made for me that hung on the back of the door.

I went into the room and riffled through the wardrobe and found tons of beautiful clothes in my size. There were dresses, slacks, and blouses in a range of styles from casual to very formal. There was also a part with underwear that put Victoria Secret to shame. I pulled out some jeans and a nice black silky shirt and some underwear and set them at the end of the bed. I then crawled back into the bed and went back to sleep. I needed some sleep and strength if I was going to save the day.

Chapter Fourteen

A New Day

When I woke up the next morning, there was a food tray next to my bed with steaming black coffee, fruit, a spinach and egg white sandwich and what I could only presume to be a cup of blood. I wondered who the blood donor was and how someone was able to bring this into my room without waking me. I was usually not a heavy sleeper, any sound would wake me which made me wonder if they had drugged me earlier or if it was related to my head injury. I touched my head to see if it was still sensitive and it seemed to have actually healed completely. Well, time to make my debut at being the perfect daughter so I could get us out of this mess. I quickly ate, leaving the blood untouched. I dressed and applied some of the cosmetics I saw on the counter. When I felt ready, I made my way downstairs.

"Well, I know you're not happy to see me but I am beyond thrilled to see you my friend." Lindsey smirked. I wanted to punch her in the face again, but instead I ignored her and walked on past. Surprisingly, she didn't try to follow me. I would never trust her again so I don't know why she even bothered.

I walked into a room that I suppose you could call a living room but it was about as large as my new family's living room. It didn't feel very homey, instead it was filled with expensive antiques and furniture that didn't look very comfortable at all. Everything in there was for looks only. Julian was sitting there with a very pretty woman that looked to be in her mid-thirties but with Crissnas it was hard to tell her true age. She rose when I entered the room and puckered her lips like she had just finished sucking on a lemon. She changed her expression to be one of welcome and introduced herself as Olivia.

"I am so happy to meet you Phoebe. Your father here has been waiting for this reunion for much too long. I will let you two get back to getting acquainted." She looked back at Julian and nodded and then left the room. I walked in and awkwardly sat on one of the sofas. I was right, they were uncomfortable. "So father, what would you like to talk about?"

He raised his eyebrows in surprise. "I just want to know everything about you Phoebe. Tell me about your life with your mom."

Bringing up my mom made tears sting the back of my eyes, but I was not going to let him see that. "Life with mom was good. She was always there for me. When I was little, we would bake together and play board games. Her favorite was mancala. She used to love to make arts and crafts and we would spend hours making candles or soaps. She was also very artistic. She used to draw pictures which she called doodles but I thought should be displayed in art galleries. She always said it was a way for her to keep her anxiety at bay. She was a very anxious person but now I understand why. She was keeping a very big secret. As I got older, she would stay up and help me with my homework and wait up for me after band parties."

"You were in the band?"

"Yes, I played the clarinet and I was also the color guard captain. It was honestly the only part of school that I really enjoyed. I never felt like I really fit. I tried to find my place, but I was just socially awkward and I would beat myself up for doing or saying the wrong thing so after a while I stopped trying. Then Lindsey came along and I thought I had hit the jackpot because she was the best friend anyone could ask for. I wish I knew back then that she was just using me to find out everything she could and answer back to you. It just makes me feel very betrayed." My throat began to clog and my voice sounded heavy, even to my ears. "Mom passed away and life changed dramatically. I finished college and went to work as an editor and I write my own books on my own time and that is really my life in a nutshell. I am not terribly interesting."

"Oh, I find you very intriguing. What was it like growing up with the human man that your mom married?" he said with great distaste.

"He was distant most of the time. He never really showed love to me or mom. I often wondered why she married him. Mom was so full of life and so happy all the time. He was her polar opposite. He would go to work, come home and eat, and then he would plop himself on the couch and watch t.v. for the rest of the evening ignoring both of us. I understand now why he treated me like that but why did mom put up with it? I will never understand their dynamic. He and I don't speak anymore, not really at all since mom died. It was like his only reason for tolerating me was gone so he stopped pretending even a little bit."

It still hurt, thinking about the way I was always treated. I wanted Julian to trust me so I gave him the entire truth leaving nothing out. I needed him to believe in me so I could start seeing Xander on a regular basis and he and I could figure a way out of Pandora's box.

"I am sorry for the way you were treated. If I had been there, things would have been different. Neither you nor your mother would have ever been ignored and neither of you would have wanted for anything. I would have given you both the world. As it is, I will spend the rest of my days giving you everything your heart desires to make up for it."

I inwardly cringed because I knew it was nothing but a load of lies, but I bit my tongue and smiled instead.

"Do you like horses, Phoebe?"

"I love horses. Mom and I used to go to this stable and go horseback riding every summer."

"After it gets dark this evening, would you like to go out and ride the horses with me? I have one that is especially beautiful and docile that I think you will like."

"Of course. Will Xander be joining us?"

"I believe he has other items on his agenda."

I tried to reach out with my mind to find Xander but could not feel him at all in the house. I started to worry that Julian had done something to him but I didn't get that feeling from him. I hoped that Xander was ok. I needed to work my magic on Julian fast so I could get to him and at least assure myself that he was going to be alright.

My mind began wandering to Alaric and the rest of the family and how they must be feeling. I suddenly felt a tickling at the fringes of my mind. At first, I wasn't sure what it was and then I felt a whisper of a thought from Alaric. He was frantically wondering where we were. I remembered I was still in Julian's presence and looked up in time to see him studying me like I was an insect and he wasn't sure if he wanted to study me or squash me. The emotion was fleeting before the smile was plastered back on his face.

"I need to go out and do a little business today. I am sure my staff will do their best to make you feel at home." With that, he looked over my shoulder at one of the burly guys who looked at me like he definitely wanted to end me.

I decided to throw in that extra touch to make Julian think he was making progress and took a few strides toward him and gave him a quick hug before exiting the room. I didn't look back to see his reaction but I could feel his surprise. I hoped it was the first step toward getting Xander back and gaining our freedom.

I practically ran back up to my temporary room so I could concentrate to try to get a message to Alaric. I don't know why it hadn't occurred to me before this but I blamed the head injury.

I went up and laid on the bed and tried to picture Alaric in my head without crying. I tried to tell him through our connection that we were both with Julian at his home. I could still feel his frantic emotions but I could not seem to concentrate hard enough to get my message through. After hours of trying, I began to get a migraine and my stomach reminded me I hadn't eaten yet today.

I really wanted to find Xander and make sure he was surviving but I didn't want to break what little trust I may have gained with Julian. I trotted downstairs and placed the fake smile on my face and asked one of the Arnold impersonators where I might find some food. He grunted and nodded in a direction which I followed. Apparently, he was hired for his brawn and not his brains.

As I walked through the halls of the house and peeked into each room downstairs, every room was just like its owner. The walls were painted dark colors, the furnishings were old and stiff, and there was a smell of staleness. Each room was very unlike the room I sat in with him on that first meeting, with its cheery colors and natural lighting. The rest of the house felt like a tomb.

I finally reached the kitchen and while it was dark like the rest of the house, the smells wafting through the air made it seem more alive. My stomach began to grumble at the scent and the thought of food. There were a few women in there cooking. They all seemed wary of me, like I had the plague and touching me would transfer it to them. I tried to seem cheerful as I asked for some food.

At first, they just looked at each other like they were not sure what they should do. Then, the sturdiest of them came forward. She was wearing her brown hair tied up in a bun and a large white apron around her body. She was holding a wooden spoon and pointed it at me as she asked what I would like.

"I am happy with anything, really. It smells like heaven here in the kitchen." I replied with a smile and that seemed to take her out of her grimace. Slowly, she began to smile back at me and I felt like just maybe I was making a new friend here. She grabbed a board and began to pile it with little sandwiches, fruits, and a wide array of raw vegetables. Either Julian had been studying me and knew what I preferred or this was just a happy coincidence. She set it down in front of me with a large tumbler of water.

"Is there anything else I can get for you?"

I placed my hand on her sleeve."Thank you so much. This looks delicious." She seemed surprised by the way I was reacting and her smile inched up and she quickly went back to work. The rest of the ladies followed suit as I quickly scarfed down my food.

When I was finished, I asked if there was anything I could do to help cook or clean up and this earned a smile from all of them.

"Of course not. You are Julian's guest. You run along and enjoy your day." As I left the smile left her face and there was a fleeting look of concern before I turned and strode away. I quietly pondered what that might be about. Did she not like Julian? Maybe she would end up being an ally, someone that could help us find our way out of this mess.

I was startled by the door opening and Julian gallantly walking through like he was some kind of knight in shining armor. He was dressed in a white riding outfit which seemed very out of place on him.

"Are you ready to go riding now, my dear?"

I had all but forgotten about our conversation that morning.

"Of course, let's go."

We walked onto the grounds out to the stables and I inconspicuously looked around trying to find any possible ways out once I had rescued Xander. The house seemed to be surrounded by nothing but a heavily wooded area. I strained to hear any sounds of life outside of his compound but I could hear nothing. No cars, no people, just nothing. That didn't bode well for us having an easy way to get out of here.

The stables were filled with horses of every size and color. They were absolutely beautiful and there were several stable hands out there taking great care of them. I was pleasantly surprised. I rode a beautiful black stallion named Stavos. His coat was shiny and his mane was gorgeous. He was not the docile horse named Lucy that Julian wanted me to ride. I was an experienced rider so I wanted a horse with some power. Julian would have preferred that I have one that can't go too far too fast. He was just going to have to trust me.

We rode around the compound and it was just as I originally thought, there did not seem to be any roads near his monstrosity of a home. That would not take away my hope. Our horses galloped around and he tried to make small talk. I smiled when appropriate but truthfully his voice and his very being just got under my skin. I was certain that if he was my father, I completely understood why my mother got as far away from him as possible. He had an arrogant air about him and gave me the impression he considered me more of a possession than a daughter. I tried to keep that mental wall up around me so that if he could hear my thoughts they would be the ones he wanted to hear. Unfortunately, he seemed to have the same wall because I could not hear his thoughts or channel his feelings.

If I were here for any other reason and here with people who didn't make my skin crawl, then I would be able to enjoy the serene surroundings. The trees were so lush, the land so beautiful that it could take your breath away. It was so peaceful with the sounds of birds chirping and animals scampering around the woods enjoying their lives oblivious to the evil that resided on this land.

I again wondered about Xander and if they were treating him like a guest and not a prisoner.

"Father, when do you think I might be able to see Xander? I would at least like to talk to him and see that he is faring well." I tried to leave the hatred out of my voice that I was beginning to feel for this man.

He looked at me with that fake smile plastered on his face. If he was at all surprised by me calling him father he didn't show it. "Soon dear. I just want to give you time to become acclimated with us and your real family before seeing him again. I want you to realize we are the ones being wronged here." He almost sounded convincing but there were warning bells going off in my head that something was very wrong with Xander. It was like I could almost hear Xander's whispered voice telling me to leave and save myself. I attributed it to an overactive imagination and tried with all my energy to look contrite.

"Of course. I understand and I am happy to stay with you. You can go ahead and let him go then. There is no need for him to be here since I am staying and getting to know you."

He ignored me as if I had never spoken at all which made me feel like my blood was suddenly over a hundred degrees and boiling inside my skin. I could feel my face getting hot and it took all my control to keep my blue fire from erupting from my entire being. I could see it in my mind as if it were happening. He was screaming as my fire consumed him until he was nothing, until he was ash.

He rode ahead a bit and was pointing out some of the fauna in the area and making sure I understood just how remote his homestead was. While pretending to be the perfect host, what he was really drilling home is that I had no chance for escape. Suddenly the only thing I wanted to do was burn every last bit of it down.

When we got back, I gave the excuse that I was tired to get back to my room and away from him before I really did murder him. I knew that I could do it but I was also aware that his minions would end me and worse Xander. I needed to see Xander. That was my first mission, the next was to find a way out of this hell.

I was a planner. I usually wrote down everything I needed to from step A through Z. My plan was to watch and observe over the next day or so everyone's routines day and night. I needed to meticulously check out each room in this beautifully crafted place of confinement until I found the one containing Xander. I thought about how scared he must be and how worried he had to be about the rest of the family.

I knew they were doing everything they could to find us and I had a lot of confidence in that but Alaric's voice was just a distant whisper in my head so I knew he wasn't making any gains. I could hear his whispers and torturous thoughts about what may have happened to me and to his brother. I wondered if he could feel my thoughts at all from so far away. Our bond was strong in such a short time. I already missed the way he held me so tight when he would hug me. The way it felt to be in his arms, so safe, protected, and loved. I had never had that with any man before and I longed for the day he would be able to wrap his strong arms around me again.

That night, I crept out of my room. My door opened with a slight creek and I waited what seemed like hours to make sure no one heard me. The hall was dark and silent. I was wearing the soft robe that my seemingly generous and wicked father had left out for me. My soft footsteps barely made a sound on the cold floors and I tiptoed around. Before I opened any doors, I stood behind them straining to hear any noise. My fear was opening a door and instead of finding Xander, finding one of my father's minions, Lyndsey, or worse my father. Any of them would put a speedy stop to my midnight travels.

I began quietly opening doors only to find opulently decorated rooms with silks and fine furnishings but not a person in sight. Out of nowhere, I could feel a humming in my core. It was like an invisible cord was pulling me in the opposite direction. Was this some sort of Crissna trick or were my own instincts trying to assist me? I decided to trust the feeling, it didn't feel evil, but like it was a part of me.

This cord led me downstairs. I should have been afraid that I would be discovered but my mind was assured and confident. It didn't make any sense but I felt sure that I was going to find Xander and not encounter any trouble on my way. My path led me down a dank corridor that smelled of must and rot. It was hard to believe this was even a part of the elaborately decorated and gorgeous house. It felt like I was entering a tunnel of sorts and I had to duck a bit to continue and I was not terribly tall so this was very short. The dark cozy tunnel was not mixing well with my claustrophobia. It forced me to stop for a moment and close my eyes. I took a deep breath of moldy air and concentrated on the humming and pulling in my center and walked on. There was a wooden door that looked like it had not been opened in ages. Surely Xander was not there but that pull was telling me to open it. The door opened inch by inch without a sound. What I saw knocked the breath out of me.

Xander was splayed out on a cot not fit for a rodent. The room was tiny and the walls were made from old brick that once was probably red but was now were so covered with dirt and mold their color was indistinguishable. Blood was spread in patterns across the cold concrete floor and there was so much I feared that Xander was no longer alive. His eyelids did not even flutter when I rushed over to him. The rough gray wool blanket that covered him rubbed my hands like sandpaper as I leaned over him to touch his cheek.

His skin was as pale as I had always imagined that a Vampire's should be if I believed all the books and legends. It didn't look as though any spark of life still resided there. As the tears pricked the inside of my eyelids, his hand moved just the slightest bit. I kneeled down. "Xander, can you hear me?"

Finally, his eyes opened just a fraction, enough for me to rejoice that he was still alive. I couldn't help but lean over him and hold him. The relief was like a living breathing entity. His arm came up and held me weakly in place. "What did they do to you?"

His words came out slowly as the strain for him to speak was in every syllable. "They made me drink something. I don't know what it was but I felt powerless and drained. They beat me within an inch of my life and no one has come back since."

"Why aren't you healing? I thought we healed fast."

"Whatever was in that concoction is like nothing I have ever known because I feel almost human. Every part of me hurts."

His eyes fluttered shut again. If he had been down here for this long and no one had come back, he had not eaten or drank anything. "Zander, I am going to go and get you some food and something to clean you up. I don't dare try to get you out of here yet but I promise I will. I will be back." I touched his cheek briefly once more and I fled the room. I followed my way back up to the main home and into the kitchen to scrounge up anything I could. I found a first aid kit while I was there which would prove useful. I grabbed some bread, cheese, and a thermos of water assuming those were the items they would be likely to miss the least. I dribbled some blood from a couple of steaks that were in the fridge and added it to a cup. I then scurried back down to the depths of the home to take care of Xander.

This time he opened his eyes. I set the food next to him and I helped him to get into a sitting position so he could eat, I gave him some water and it looked like it hurt him just to swallow. While he ate, I tried to survey the damage. He had bruises that were beginning that ugly yellow brown stage all over his very naked abdomen. I prayed to God that he had on some pants underneath that awful excuse for a blanket. His abs were chiseled by God himself and his biceps were much larger than I had imagined. He was breathtaking despite all the blood and bruises that coated his body.

When he was finished with his food, I pulled out the first aid kit and began cleaning up what I could. Most of what was left were bruises and nothing in that kit was going to help with that. He brushed aside the blanket to survey the damage himself and luckily still had on his pants and even his shoes. I cleaned up the dried blood and aside from the bruises he looked almost whole again.

"I am going to get you out of here. I promise. There didn't seem to be anyone awake in the house so when we get out of here it will have to be in the middle of the night and we will need our speed which is something I don't think you have right now. I will come and visit you every night and bring you food until you have enough strength to escape with me."

He touched my arm and his touch with feather light. He looked at me and his eyes were a liquid brown, I felt like I could see right down to his soul. "I want you to go, Phoebe. My only care is that you are safe. Don't look back and don't come back for me. As long as you are ok, that is the only thing in the world that matters and if you stay here you won't be. I heard things when they were outside my door right before they did this to me. They have a plan to use you somehow and I can't have that." Each word seemed like it strained his body to say.

At that moment, my heart felt like it was in my throat and I could not speak. I began to sob and hold him as tightly as I could without harming him more. "Xander, you are important to me and I will not leave here without you. I am getting us both out of here as soon as I can. Don't give up on yourself right now or ever." I felt a whisper in my head that told me to leave now so I didn't get caught. "Look. I have to get back upstairs but I will come back."

With that, I grabbed the thermos and hid it under his bed so he could have water later and took the first aid supplies and vanished. I put the kit back where I found it and got back up to my room before I heard someone wandering the halls. I held my breath to see if I had been discovered and exhaled when I heard the footfalls go past and not stop.

I vowed at that moment as soon as Xander was ready, I would get him out of here even if I had to sacrifice myself.

The days seemed endless and all I could look forward to was getting to see Xander at midnight when the household was asleep. During the days, I spent time with my father as he tried to impress me with being the best father he could be. We rode the horses daily and I became quite attached to my horse. I felt sorry that the horse was stuck in this household. He would have elaborate meals at a dining room table that looked like it was not touched on any other occasions.

I didn't see Lindsey and I wondered if she was still even around. That was one small blessing at least. I saw the Arnold minions creeping around the house often and staring daggers at me. I knew that if my father allowed it they would make sure I was murdered in my sleep.

I tried to read their minds daily to see what their ultimate plans were but they must have known about my abilities because I could never tell what exactly was going on. Xander had overheard them saying I had some purpose and I knew in my heart the purpose was not to be a great daughter but to be some tool utilized in the way they saw fit. I just wish I knew what that was exactly.

I was biding my time until I could make my escape with Xander in tow. I would make my way back to the family and back to safety however possible.

At night, I would sneak food down to Xander and each time I saw him, he began to look better and better. We would discuss our escape plan and in those stolen moments we began to form a bond that I knew would be unbreakable.

""How was today? I know it is not easy for you to endure being around all of them." Xander asked as he munched on some leftovers from dinner. I brought him pieces of filet mignon and a leftover baked potato. My father spared no expense in trying to dazzle me.

I was always so amazed that this man who had fought for me, was injured because of me, and was stuck in what was no better than a dungeon, was more concerned about me. He would stare at me with those chocolate brown eyes and hold my hand as we talked about our likes and dislikes, our futures after all of this. He would even bring up how happy Alaric would be to see me even though I knew deep down it hurt him to say that.

After that first night, I had managed to bring him down a wash bowl, some soap, and a toothbrush. I also swiped some clothing from the wardrobe of one of the Arnold minions for him so he could feel a little less disgusting. Instead of thanking me right away he seemed upset. He didn't want me taking any chances just to make him more comfortable.

I came to realize that Xander was one of the most caring people I had ever met. He was a lot like his mom, always trying to look after me despite his own situation. He often encouraged me to leave without him to save myself.

I actually found myself laughing with him quite a bit despite our circumstances. He was so easy to be around, I would stay for a few hours at a time and not even realize where the time had gone. He was a lot like me, he loved books, he loved pets and children. We enjoyed a lot of the same types of movies and genre of books even. I envied him for his childhood and siblings though. The way he talked about each of them and the way they all grew up, he would smile from his eyes and get a far off look. His love for each of them was clear and his worry that he would not see them again was evident as well. I wanted to put his mind at ease and let him know that getting him out of there was my priority but he would just get frustrated telling me to save myself.

Chapter Fifteen

The Breaking Point

Time went on like this for a few weeks and as each day passed Xander began to feel more himself. I believe he had broken a rib but it was almost healed and slowly his powers seemed to be coming back so whatever they gave him was at least not a permanent elixir. I knew it would not be long before we could get out of there.

It was long after dinner, around the time I sequestered myself into my borrowed room when I had a restless feeling. I felt that invisible cord again pulling me out and downstairs. I followed it out to the stables and no one stopped me from going out there by myself. My father must have started to trust me which could work in my favor. I hadn't asked to see Xander anymore and I remained as cheerful and interested in my father as possible when he was around.

I began to walk near the door of the stable and my intuition told me to stop. It was as though an invisible hand had reached out and grabbed me around the waist tightening its grip to keep me safe. I stood just outside in the shadows and waited. My heart was pounding in my chest and I could feel each breath. I felt a sense of dread and my patience was soon rewarded. I could hear my father's voice and a woman that sounded like the one I had met when I was first brought here.

"You need to work faster. She needs to completely trust you. It has been weeks and you are not making the progress that he expects!"

"I have made a lot of progress. She isn't even asking about that damn rat we have in the basement anymore. He is probably dead by now with that beating he took after swallowing half a cup of that potion you provided. He won't be a problem."

"You better make sure he is not a problem. We need to get her to agree to show us her powers. We know she is the one the prophecy is about. She could change everything but if we don't have her on our side, she can eradicate us, all of us. So work harder!"

With that, the voices faded and I moved further into the shadows away from prying eyes. Xander and I had to get out of there and tonight or they would kill him. No more time for planning. It was time for action. Since I was so important to their plan they wouldn't dare kill me. As long as I could get Xander out of there, I could figure out the rest later.

A bit before midnight, I went down to the dungeon to rescue Xander. I hurried in and when he saw I didn't bring anything with me he shot up off the cot. "What is it? What's wrong?""We have to get out of here now. I overheard my so-called father talking and our time is up."

Xander grabbed my hands and looked at me as if he could see straight into my soul. "No matter what happens. I want you to get out of here. If anything happens, you save yourself, do you understand me?" His intense focus was no longer on my eyes but my lips and I Knew what was going to happen. I loved Alaric and I knew I shouldn't allow it but something inside of me broke loose. It was like I needed him and the comfort he offered.

He leaned in slowly, giving me time to protest and when I didn't, his lips were like butterfly wings barely touching mine at first. It was a whisper of a kiss. He leaned back and took one more hesitant look and then crushed his lips against mine. I didn't expect to feel the spark of emotion that I did. It wasn't like kissing Alaric but it felt right. I could feel his thoughts like a light brush against my senses. I could feel how much he loved me and wanted to keep me safe. My lips parted and his kiss seared me. I knew somewhere in the recesses of my mind that there was a part of me that cared for him deeply. Maybe even a small part that loved him too. After a moment I broke off the kiss and held on to him for a few seconds longer then let go.

"We are both going to make it out of here Xander."

We headed up into the house with me leading the way and stopping every few seconds to make sure the house was still quiet. We made it as far as the door when the man that claimed to be my father turned on the light. Standing next to him were two of the three minions looking ready to murder both of us. Xander immediately stood in front of me.

"Let her go! You are never going to be able to leave your home again if you hurt her because my family will hunt you to the ends of the earth."

Julian laughed like Xander was doing a stand up comedy act and had just said the most hilarious thing. "Do you really think I am worried about your pathetic family? Be serious."

I tried to step around Xander but he sidestepped me easily. "I know that you need me alive for your prophecy. I also know that you are not my father! Let him go and then I will stay."

Julian seemed a little taken aback from that. Then he showed his evil grin and ushered his minions forward. "Kill him. Then put her in his place in the basement."

Xander looked like he was ready to put up the fight of his life for me. I could feel him calling out to me pleading with me to run.

In that moment, everything began to happen in slow motion. I could see the grotesque smirk on Julian's face and the echo of his laughter rickocketing around the room. His minions rushed forward but looked as though they were stuck in molasses as they slowly moved to grab Xander. I watched as Xander slowly turned around toward me to push me out of the way. I could hear a clock somewhere in the monsorous house chiming down to midnight and the sound reverberated in my soul.

Something inside of me clicked. It was not a subtle feeling, but one of power rushing through to me from every fiber of my being and pulsating in the air around me. I could feel it starting at my toes and fingers and moving into the center of my being like being lit by a bolt of electricity and being fed by it instead of perishing from it.

My entire body began to levitate from the ground and blue sparks surrounded me. Everyone stopped. Xander stopped and stared in awe, not bothering to see if the men were still coming for him. The men stopped in mid-run toward us and began to cower in fright. Julian finally stopped his maniacal laughing and looked like someone had punched the oxygen right out of his lungs.

As for me, I felt more powerful than I ever had. I could feel every nerve ending was alive and my anger for Julian and the others was a monster gnawing inside of me waiting to be released. When the clock finally hit that last stroke to signal midnight, my body unleashed all that anger. A silver shield formed around Xander as all of my blue midnight fire consumed everything and everyone else. The men were first to be consumed, one moment they were cowering in front of me and the next they were nothing but ash floating in the maelstrom of wind that was created by my power. Julian was next and I had never felt so vindicated as I did when he was no more. The draperies and rugs began to catch flame and everything went up in a crackling blue fire as I floated above it all and watched it burn.

Within minutes, there was nothing left but Xander and I. His protective shield began to dissolve and my body slowly lowered until my feet were once again the only things holding me aloft. The wind died down and my light left me and I looked at Xander in amazement. He looked like he had just seen something amazing that he couldn't quite believe. We were the last two people in a universe of crazy that left us with nothing but the peaceful trees and grass around us.The stables were still intact and I could feel the horses and every other insect and animal around me. I could feel the blades of grass slowly unwinding from the earth and the trees growing and soaking up the water from the soil. It was like I was connected to everything. I could feel Xander and his energy vibrating around me and toward me. I could feel his awe and overpowering feelings for me as if I could reach out and touch them. I could see the invisible cord now visible and shining silver connecting us to one another. It was almost like my recurring dream where he stands there with his arms open waiting to welcome me home.

I ran to him and he hugged me tightly. He was the beacon of calm within my storm. I could feel his sense of awe at what I had done and his relief that I was safe. He also had a sense of possessiveness of me, of wanting to take care of me forever that shook me to my core. I knew that I loved him but there was Alaric and his love was a brand on my soul that could never be replaced. I began to break away from Xander when suddenly I could feel Alaric. Xander stiffened as I backed away and his eyes peered to a place past me.

I turned in time to see Alaric just passing the last tree that marked the edge of the woods and the path to me. We ran to each other, lips colliding, limbs grasping. The fire I felt in his arms was all consuming. His kiss told me the story of how much he was worried and so relieved to see me safe. The world around us no longer existed, it was just him and I and our love for each other. I kept kissing him afraid that if I stopped, I would realize it was all an illusion and I was given the same potion Xander was and this was my hallucination.

"I love you. I could feel your rage and I was finally able to find you. I just kept running towards the feeling of you, hoping I was right and I would finally find you."

"You're here? You are really here? I can't believe it. I love you!"

"I love you too Phoebes. It is all going to be ok now."

The rest of the family rushed past the tree line, all three of them taking in everything. Alyssa ran to Xander, who was forgotten in the rush I felt upon seeing Alaric. She squeezed him tight and then ran to us to do the same. Belle was crying and hugged us all while Steve looked relieved and pulled the entire family together.

I was overwhelmed. There were so many emotions flooding my system that I wasn't sure which held the forefront. I was relieved that it was all over and not only did I keep Xander safe but also made it out myself. I had sometimes let myself wonder if I would ever see Alaric and the rest of the family again. I was so overwhelmed with love for all of them that I felt like crying and laughing at the same time. The fact that I could do what I just did gave me pause and made me wonder what I was and what I was truly capable of. The prophecy that my fake father had spoken of had me awash in dread and concern over what it was and what my part in it was. Then there was my love for Xander and my relief that he was ok being overshadowed by my reunion with Alaric. Like Scarlett O'Hara, I would have to think about that another day. It was time to go home, rest, recoup, and there would be time later for all the heavy.

EPILOGUE

Two months had passed since the day we came back home. After forty eight hours of solid sleep, while Alaric watched over me dutifully, the family began to comb through the ashes of what had occured. We went back to the scene to see if we could find any clues about the prophecy but everything and everyone was gone with my midnight fire. I often wondered if Lindsey was in the house when I turned it into nothing. Did she feel anything when she died? Who was Julian and what part did he have in what was to come? How did I have the power to eradicate an entire race and why would I when not all of them were living their lives to hurt others? What was I truly, since Vampires only had one major ability besides speed, and immortality?

It seemed like we were no closer to answering any of this than we were the day we left the mansion. We would need to continue to pull all of our resources and time to find out the answers. Other Crissnas were behind this, Julian was just a pawn in the larger game. I had no idea who else was involved or who my father really was and if he had anything to do with any of this. There was no doubt that they would continue to come after me so we all decided it was time to move on to another state, another town, and blend in while we tried to figure this out.

We moved to California, in a little town called Tulare. It was out in the country a bit and we tried to blend in but always stayed on the lookout for the Crissnas and whoever was behind our kidnapping. The family moved into a very large home with three stories. There was about an acre cleared around the home but the rest was wooded and offered us an inconspicuous way for me to continue to try out new powers and see what I could do without prying eyes.

Alaric and I moved into a smaller cabin on the estate so we could have our privacy. Ever since we had come home, the cord between Xander and I, while still there, had become dimmer for me. He still owned a place in my heart and I still had not told Alaric what had happened between us. I told myself it was to save their relationship. The truth was, I was not ready to really face what had happened or how strong my feelings to protect him had been.

So for now, I would stay in my protective bubble with Alaric, savoring the feel of his love. We spent every moment possible together, our nights were hot and I never grew tired of that. We dreamed about a time when we were past all the craziness of whatever this prophecy was and past people hunting me. We dreamed and romanticized about all the adventures we would have together and even talked about forever.

Neither of us were prepared for what came next.

The End...for now.

About Author

Author Nicole Osborne lives in the Western U.S. with her husband. Her adult children and grandchildren live near and she loves spending time with her family. When she is not hiking or spending time outdoors, she is finding quiet places to read and write. She loves to travel to other countries and learn about other cultures. She can be reached on her webpage www.NicoleOsborneauthor.com. You will also find her on Facebook Nicole Osborne author and on TikTok @NicoleOsborneauthor.

Also By

Nicole also has a serial killer series

The Savior- The Story of a Serial Killer
Revenge- The Story of a Serial Killer
More Coming soon...

Blue Midnight
(Blue Midnight series- book 2- title TBA- coming soon).